GIANT HUNTER

A NOVELLA BY

LLOYD TACKITT

FOREWORD:

At age fourteen Robert Hunter's safe and comfortable world is turned upside-down. A stranger rode into his life and destroyed all that he held dear. Robert, an intelligent but naïve youth, sets out to right this terrible wrong. Along the way he is confronted, once again, by the menace of the mutant giants that roam the world at will, destroying men and all they've managed to rebuild after a colossal meteor storm had all but wiped out civilization. His mission is put on hold after he becomes suddenly aware that he is quite possibly the only person that has the skills and knowledge to put a stop to the giant's rampages.

This novella is preceded by the short story "Giants", available on Amazon.

GIANT HUNTER

I WATCHED THE GIANTS FROM BEHIND some brush. Thin brush. They were a long way off and I had spotted them by the dust they were kicking up. I'd say the bottom of the valley was three miles from me and there was a large impact crate between us, but giants have keen senses and they are so fast they could cross those three miles and the crater before I could run a half mile. So I was a little nervous, and fatalistic. I didn't think they would spot me, but if they did I'd be dead in minutes. That was an absolute certainty.

I let them get out of sight, and I waited until I couldn't feel the thundering of their feet through the earth. And then I waited the rest of the night, since it had gotten dark while I waited. I didn't build a fire though. I counted myself lucky to spend a cold night huddled under a blanket and shivering. Very lucky.

Had I not stopped to drink at the last creek, and I wasn't all that thirsty but you don't pass up opportunities when you're riding into places you've never been, I'd have ridden right into them. That extra time allowed me to spot them before they spotted me, and that was all the difference there was between me being alive and feeling the cold or being a headless bag of shriveled skin. It was that close, and it was a thing completely out of my control.

Dying would have been bad enough. It would have been brutal but at least fast. But I was on a mission, and if I didn't complete that mission, those short brutal last seconds of death would have hurt far worse.

I was tracking the man that murdered my parents. Fourteen years old and my life had one burning focus. Find him, kill him. Nothing else mattered at all. Absolutely nothing else mattered to me. Nothing at all.

Pa was a rancher in west Texas. He was an inventor of things, mostly steam driven things. Pa had a great mind, one that never sensed a limitation on what he could accomplish. Ma was loving, sweet, and gentle – and seriously stubborn. Pa had become famous and wealthy after inventing a machine that would kill the giants. The first machine of its kind. Pa and I were the first to ever kill a giant, as a matter of fact. This had brought a lot of fame and gold from the killing machines we built for others. Giants were a severe problem, and up until Pa took it on, it had been a problem without a solution.

The gold that rolled in from making more of those machines was incredible. People showed up at our door with bags of gold, just begging to buy one of the giant killers. So Pa and I began building the machines, and improving on them as we went. Eventually other people started to manufacture the machines using assembly line processes, and from places that had more resources than we had. So the price of the machines began to fall and reached a point where we couldn't compete. Pa told me he was real happy about that too. He was tired of building the same thing over and over. I know I was so I'm sure he must have been twice as tired of it as me. Pa was an inventor, not an assembly line worker. He was happy to be free of the constraints imposed by building the same thing over and over. He started smiling a lot more when he got back to inventing new things. But he would still build the giant killer machines for people that asked him to. Those people were getting farther and fewer between though.

Pa said that we had accumulated enough gold to live ten lifetimes anyway, and "We sure as hell didn't need any more of it." We had been self-sufficient before the gold, it was just a bonus, and we hardly ever spent any of it – we didn't need to. That gold was what must have drawn the killer. I'd been out checking on cattle for four days and came home to find Pa, shot in the back, and lying in the yard. Ma was dead in the kitchen, shot in the face. The killer had taken a bag of gold coins from the house; he didn't find the big stash inside one of the machines in the barn.

Pa's sense of humor knew few boundaries. He had melted some of the gold down and minted his own, unique coins – since there was no official nation to issue official currency, everyone pretty much worked on the barter system, but gold was spendable anywhere and could be pretty handy to have around. Pa cast his gold coins with a giant on one side and his machine on the other. Each coin was scored deeply into eight sections, so that a piece could be broken off by bending it back and forth;

making each coin into eight smaller pie-shaped ones. It was an idea from the "pieces of eight" Pa had read about.

It took me a week to bury my folks and make arrangements to go after their murderer. First thing I did was to move the bodies into the living room and clean them up and cover them before the burial, it was a desperately hard task. I'm not ashamed to say I cried the whole time.

I buried all of the gold in four unmarked places around the ranch, and made arrangements with the neighbor ranchers to look after the place while I was gone. Our neighbors tried hard to talk me out of it, saying fourteen was too young to go off on such a quest, but nothing would dissuade me – Pa always said I took after Ma in the stubbornness department.

After that I went scouting, looking for any sign of the killer in case he was still close. I found horse tracks leading north, but they disappeared quickly due to the hard-pan soil and the constant blowing wind. At least I had a direction, and I knew he would spend those coins he stole, and I had an idea people would remember him for that.

My neighbors gathered and we dug a double grave up on a small hill overlooking the house. The wind that blows constantly in west Texas had died down to a whisper, dark clouds hanging low, dropping slow fat drops of rain in a steady sprinkle. We placed my parents in the single grave, together, holding hands in the extra wide coffin I'd built. We had a fine preacher, a neighbor whose deep baritone voice lifted and swelled and ended with "dust to dust" in a near whisper to match the wind. I had never thought about those words, although I was familiar with them. Now I did, and saw the truth of it, their glorious lives that they had lived with so much love and promise were forever gone, and only dust would remain of them. Dust and memories.

There was lots of singing and our voices carried out over the plains and faded away, and fittingly started a lone coyote to howling for a moment. After the service we all sat down to eat, the feast my neighbors had brought, as people do at funerals out here. There were a lot of stories told about Ma and Pa, and I teared up more than once. The pain of grief came in waves, washing over me and leaving me gasping and crying, then passing on again leaving a lasting hollow sadness. When the last hug had been given and the final attempts at lifting my burden had gone silent, after the last neighbor had gone home, I saddled up and began the hunt. I was fairly chafing to get going but sending my folks off in the right way had to come first. Now that they had been buried as well as anyone I'd ever heard tell of, it was time to get after their killer.

I retraced where I'd lost the tracks, searched hard for two days and found one more track, a rock, scarred from his horse's steel shoe. It's hard land, all edges, and nearly all the time windy. The plants that grow here mostly have thorns and are made of tough wood. The scrub trees looked like metal sculptures from a twisted mind. Impact craters were scattered randomly across the land, as they were everywhere on the planet now. Living off that land tends to make for hard people, but people with big hearts for all the hardships they faced every day. Pa had called them "Iron people" because soft people didn't stay or survive. The track I found was still going north. I rode the horse at a jog following the line I had, waiting to encounter other people, people I could ask questions of. And I asked everyone I could find, which weren't a lot – he seemed to avoid folks that lived out of town, but sometimes rode into a town spending some of that gold in a saloon or hotel. Over time I eventually got a fairly complete description of the man. Mostly from town people.

People are peculiar; what gets their attention is often some odd ball little thing, something out of the ordinary of their repetitive lives. Those coins were odd, so everyone who got paid with that gold remembered the man that spent it. Slowly the description built until I knew I was searching for a man in his mid-to-late thirties, six feet tall, one-hundred-eighty pounds. He had long brown hair, mud-brown eyes and a scar about an inch long just under his left eye. He rode a bay horse with a plain saddle. He packed a six gun on his hip like he knew how to use it, a lever action rifle in the saddle boot. They all said he had a hard look about him. They all said they were glad to see him go.

People didn't cotton to him. He was rude, surly. Didn't talk much, but when he did he seemed to be insulting someone as though he was daring a fight. People in these days don't relish fighting with strangers, there's no percentage in it. But he did find one man that pushed back, up in the Panhandle, near old Amarillo. They say he drew and fired so fast the other man had barely gotten his gun out of his holster before he was down. One thing he never seemed to do was mention his own name. I don't know why, but I sorely wanted to put a name to him, as though getting his name would define him somehow.

In each town I would ask around until I knew as much as they had to pass on, the most important parts being which way he rode out and how long ago. I've been tracking him from town to town and best I can tell I'm about a month behind him now. It's been slow slogging, but lately I've been gaining, little by little. Sooner or later I'll find him, kill him, and go back home to ranch. That was the plan, the only plan I had.

Since the hell storm of huge meteors had destroyed what was left of a fragile nation eighty-odd years ago, the country, and from all accounts the entire world, had turned into a dangerous and mean place. Before the hell storm, the civilized world had been destroyed by a solar storm that wiped out all the electricity. Slowly a new nation had been formed in the old USA, led by one of my ancestors, a legendary man named Adrian Hunter, but the hell storm destroyed that too. You can't fight the whims of the universe, and the hell storm had been just such a whim.

Most folks were decent, but they had to work extremely hard to survive – and then there was that element of humanity that doesn't want to do hard work. Bandits, raiders, outlaws, killers, they abound throughout the country. A man risked his life to strike out cross-country the way I was doing, and for a not-quite fifteen year-old carrying a large supply of gold coins, it was even more dangerous. I kept the coins in a money belt hidden under my clothes and never let anyone see it. I rode carefully, avoiding sky-lighting myself on ridges, pausing often to survey the land before me, and check behind me as well. At sunset each night I built a small fire and cooked enough food for a hot dinner and a couple of cold meals the following day, then put the fire out, ate, and moved a mile or so away to find a protected spot to sleep. Fire doesn't show so well at sunset, but the light is a beacon at night and the smoke is a signal by day. I also watched how much dust I was raising as I traveled, dust is another giveaway.

I kept one coin and some bits of coins in my pants pocket for paying for things. Even then I was real careful about who I let see that gold, you could get killed easy enough just for one of the coin bits, and if anyone knew how much I had on me my life wouldn't have been worth a nickel's worth of dog meat.

I'm not ashamed to say that I was scared an awful lot of the time in those early days – and with good reason. I was young, understandably naïve, and not too skilled at the use of my pistol. I was smart enough to know how much danger I was in, but couldn't do much about it, at least not back then, I had a job to do and I was damn sure going to do it. I practiced every day with the pistol, slowly getting a little better each day. I didn't fire it often – didn't want to waste my ammo – and when I did I quickly rode right on out to put some distance between me and where I'd made the noise. I had never seen anyone draw a gun, so I had no idea how fast – or more likely how slow – I was. It was something I considered a lot.

Friendly people were rare to find, so I was careful, as much as I could be and still ask questions. They could be the most decent people on earth, but there were too many bad men out there to be friendly to strangers. Most folks would talk to you if you approached them politely, but most often they talked to you while holding a gun. It was the smart thing to do. People who survive these days aren't dumb, because dumb equals soon dead.

I'd heard tell that the Native American Indians had more or less returned to their original life styles. It made sense, there were once again vast swaths of land uninhabited and the wildlife had increased by leaps and bounds. Nomadic tribal life, living with the land, had become viable once again. There weren't many tribes though, they were few and far between so the wars between them for hunting lands were still pretty much a thing of the past. From what I'd heard they were antagonistic to interlopers into their claimed territories and it was all around best to avoid them. Not knowing where they were, or what territories they claimed, that was a bit problematic for me. I rode up on top of a small hill and below me was an Indian village. Teepees and all. The village was less than half a mile away and I was silhouetted against the sky line, something I usually tried to avoid but sometimes you just couldn't help it.

I was riding through open grassland pocked by the occasional crater. Country that had once been prairie and then wheat fields, and was now sort of a mixture of native grasses and survivor wheat. As far as you could see grass rippled in the wind like waves on an ocean, covered by the blue upside-down bowl of a sky. It was beautiful country, big horizon county, and it made me feel small and inconsequential. Riding through it I smelled the fresh broken grass from my horse's hooves, heard the occasional metallic whirring of a grasshopper flying off, the call of a meadow lark. The wind was never still, never stopped flowing across the land. I'd watch the sun as it came up to my right, then slowly climb across the sky in an arc and finally settle below the horizon to my left. Then the stars would show up and take their turn wheeling across the sky.

I looked down at the distant village. It was as though someone had cast jewels across the prairie carpet, bright colors glowing against the green background. Smoke was rising lazily from several fires, dogs and children were running and playing. Several of the villagers spotted me as soon as I'd spotted them. I sat still in my saddle, considering what to do. If I turned around and rode off, would they follow me? Probably. Would there be a fight? I doubted that I could outrun them for long, and they would know the terrain intimately, putting me at a severe disadvantage. Plus I was heavily out-numbered. This was not a happy moment in my young life.

Or should I ride on in to the village and hope for the best? Wild scenes of being burned at the stake flickered through my mind like the flames of the fire I feared. Perhaps they would be friendly if I was friendly? Overall I had no idea of which was the better course, approach or flee. I watched them watching me for a good five minutes. No one was running for their horses, no one was shouting or shrieking war cries. But watch me they did, perhaps as curious about what I would do next as I was myself. We both waited to see what I would do. Finally, without having made a conscious choice, I clucked at my horse and gently kicked his flanks and started a calm, slow, walk down to the village. It might be a fatal mistake, then again so might running. I'd just have to see. I was following my instincts.

As I came closer, most of the ones that had been watching me so intently seemed to lose interest and return to whatever it was they had been doing, their curiosity about what I would do seemingly satisfied. A couple of men began walking towards me, stopping at the edge of the village. They were dressed in buckskins with fringes, moccasins that came to their knees, and feathers entwined in their long black hair. They looked just as I had expected them to, based on old photographs from some of my dad's books. These men and their village looked just like the photographs I'd seen of Indian life in the early 1800's. Dogs barked at me and smoke swirled from multiple fires around the camp as the wind kicked up for a moment. I counted twenty-three teepees, and guessing at four people per teepee, estimated that there were about ninety or so people living here. I could see about thirty of them. When I reached the edge of the village, I stopped twenty feet from the two that had walked out to greet me, both were carrying rifles. Young and naïve as I was

I had no idea what to do next so I sat there silently. They stared back silently. It eventually dawned on me that I'd have to make the first move, they sure weren't going to. So I asked in a loud slow voice.

"Do you speak English?"

Well that just cracked them up something awful. I didn't think they would ever stop laughing at me. I blushed and felt the fool and thought about turning around and riding away. But I stuck, and when they eventually got their breath back, the taller of the two replied.

"Yep." That's all he said, but it got the other man laughing again and then the one that spoke got to laughing again and the whole thing started all over again. And it took a while for the laughing to stop again too. I was feeling mighty small and foolish about this time, and just didn't know what to do or say.

The shorter of the two, and he wasn't short by ordinary standards, appeared to take pity on me.

"Hop down and come in, food's just about ready," he said. "You look hungry. Come on now, boy, don't be so damn bashful. We ain't gonna scalp you – least not if you mind your manners." And that started them laughing all over again. This time I laughed too, their laughter, no doubt heightened by my relief, had become infectious.

I stepped down and, leading my horse, walked up to them, stuck my hand out to shake. They both grinned at me as they shook my hand in an exaggerated manner. Apparently they were starved for amusement, and I was providing plenty.

I introduced myself. "I'm Robert Hunter, and I'm

on the trail of a man that killed my parents. I aim to kill him and then go back home to my ranch." They didn't laugh at that. Instead they gave me a whole new serious look, checking me out from head to toe with grave faces.

The tall one introduced himself and his partner. "I'm Joseph Gray Wolf and this is my little brother Johnny Hat. Aren't you a bit on the young side to be tracking a killer?"

I answered the only way I knew how. "Wouldn't you be hunting your parent's murderer if you were me?"

They liked that answer, I could tell by the satisfied looks in their eyes. "Come on Robert, let's eat," Joseph said. "I'm hungry as hell." And they turned and started to walk into the camp. I followed, leading my horse. I gathered some mildly curious looks as we walked through the camp. They led me to a teepee near the center of the camp, and they entered. I ground reined my horse and followed them inside. The last thing I expected to see were a table and chairs, granted they were folding picnic type chairs; and the table was made of planks held together by bolts with wing nuts for easy disassembly, but I'd been expecting to see buffalo robes piled up on the ground. The brothers started grinning again when they saw my expression.

Joseph turned to a pretty lady that I assumed was his wife and said, "Jen we have an honored guest for lunch. This is Robert Hunter. If I'm not mistaken he is the young giant killer we've all heard about. Robert, this is my wife Jen."

Well I was floored. Not only had my whole preconceived view of Indians and Indian life been shown to be wrong, but these people actually knew who I was. My mouth dropped open and Johnny laughed and made a gesture with his hand closing his own mouth, indicating to me that mine was hanging open. Now they were all laughing again. It was obvious that I didn't have to confirm that they had me right.

Jen said, "You two stop being rude." Then she turned to me and held out her hand, which I shook. "Just ignore these big lugs, they are victims of arrested mental development, not having matured an inch past ten years old." This with a big, loving smile cast towards them. She knew how to make a fellow feel at ease right away, and I relaxed and laughed a little.

I said, "Well Ma'am you can't really blame them. I came riding in here half scared out of my wits that I'd be burned at the stake, and then asked if they spoke English. I did give them something to laugh at, and that's a fact."

Jen smiled sweetly at me. "We get that now and then, a product of this era's people being out of touch with their own history caused mostly by their being spread so thin. Are you really the little giant killer?"

I nodded. "It was my Pa that killed the giant. It was his invention. I just helped a little here and there."

"But you stood right beside him and faced the giant, too, did you not?"

I nodded again.

"Then you are indeed a hero, and our people do

honor bravery. That much of the stereotype is true, as are many others. I am proud to have you honor us at our table young Robert the Giant Killer. Please have a seat – if we don't eat right now, this stew is going to get scalded and taste bad."

The stew was delicious, the best meal I'd had since the funeral. They asked a lot of questions that I fielded between wonderful, hot bites of stew and fresh-baked bread. I asked about the bread.

"Plenty of wheat left over from the big farming days is still growing wild. Far more than we can ever use, it's a wonderful resource for us." Jen responded.

After the meal Johnny said, "You have a great story to tell about the giant killing, and the whole village will want to hear it. Please stay with us. Tonight we'll gather the village around the big central fire and you'll be the star attraction. In fact stay with us a long as you want to, become one of the tribe if you'd like, we can use new blood from a great warrior and there are lots of pretty girls to marry." He said that in a half-joking, half-serious tone.

I locked up for a second then stuttered. "Thank you, that's an awfully tempting offer. But I have to find my parent's killer and put him down. Besides, the prettiest girl is already married." I said looking at Jen, and was rewarded by a beautiful smile. "But I'll certainly stay the night. Thank you."

Jen said, "I'll let the village know that we have a guest and who you are. They'll be excited." And she ducked out the tent flap as gracefully as anything you've ever seen. She was indeed the prettiest of the pretty girls I'd already seen.

After we ate, we walked around the village

stretching our legs and letting the food settle. I was introduced to everyone, one by one, and was unfailingly greeted with friendly smiles. These were good people, handsome and clean and friendly. They spoke their native Cherokee to each other except when I was around when they spoke in English as a form of politeness to their guest. To a person they seemed intelligent and thoughtful. They spoke with soft voices, slowly and often with long pauses. No one jumped in just to fill the pauses either, and they never talked over each other, allowing each other all the time in the world they might need to complete their thoughts. I'd not met more polite people anywhere.

At the big fire that night I was introduced and asked to tell my story. I'd learned during the day that telling my story wasn't simply a matter of telling of the giant killing, it was meant to be an auto-biography of my life, with as much detail as I cared to go into. I knew they'd sit there happily listening until the sun came up if I talked that long, they are the best listeners I've ever known. This was how they wanted to get to know me, all about me, and it was something to take hold of, that's a lot of attention to have focused on you. That much interest from that many people could go to a person's head I thought.

I stood up to talk and I soon became not the least bit nervous, I'd already met each of them, and this was more like talking to a big family now than talking to strangers. I began with a description of my Ma and Pa, of the ranch, and what an average day in our lives had been like. They listened quietly, never interrupting, and with concentration as though every word was worth hearing. I talked for an hour, taking my time, pausing occasionally to gather my thoughts. I described life on a west Texas ranch, the good clean work and the pleasures that abound everywhere if you are looking for them. I dwelled more on the pleasures than the pains, though I touched on them a bit, too.

Then I opened up and told them the things I believed and lived by. Honesty being at the top. Respect for others until they demonstrate they don't deserve it.

I told them how my parents had taught me that we can control how happy or unhappy our lives are by focusing on every good aspect of any problem you encounter. My parents were always at pains to point these traits out in the people we encountered. And they also pointed out that many people focus on the negatives and lead horrible lives as a result. They taught me to compare the happiness level of the two groups of people, and to make a rational choice on which way I'd rather live. Happy or tragic, those were pretty much the choices, and even the folks who are best at focusing on the positive might still have tragedies in their lives. I went on to explain that they taught me that the tragic path had its own rewards for those who practice it, but they are negative rewards, a difficult concept to grasp at my age, but I finally got it, although I admitted it took me a long time.

The irony of what I was saying didn't occur to me at the time; although I have no doubt these days that must have been extraordinarily apparent to my listeners who were much too polite to ever point this out to me.

When I described how Ma had told Pa that she wasn't going to leave the house and he would just have to move the giant on to another path, there was polite laughter. Ma would have loved these people and they would have loved her. When I described how Pa took it on to kill the giant I could see heads nodding up and down and looks of wonderment. When I described the actual killing moment, they were all leaning in towards me, intent on not missing a single word. And when I described coming home to find my parents bodies there were tears in my eyes, and in many of the eyes watching me.

I finished by explaining that I was tracking the killer to kill him, and then return home to live on my ranch. I added that once I was back home I would always welcome each and every one of them in the same way they had welcomed me should they ever need a new place to live, and I meant every heartfelt word of that invitation. I told them I had to leave, the man had to be killed, but that I was already saddened by the thought of leaving them, and thanked them again for their kindness and warm welcome.

When I finished, Johnny Hat stood and slowly looked at every face in the crowd. "I say that this is an honorable man, young in body, but old in spirit. I say that we are honored by his presence and his invitation to his home. I say that he is a warrior and I say that we honor ourselves by making him a member of our tribe tonight." He sat down.

Joseph Gray Wolf then stood. "Robert is young,

only fourteen years, and yet he has demonstrated bravery in the very face of a giant. We've had our troubles with giants and we know what truly terrible monsters they are. Not one of us has killed a giant, but Robert has and at the age of twelve. His parents were murdered by an evil spirit, and at the age of fourteen this young warrior is following the honorable path of tracking that evil to destroy it. He is a peaccful man, only wanting to return home and live in peace, yet he first takes on the rightful challenge of ending the evil that destroyed his family. I say we give him a tribal name, Little Giant Killer."

One by one most of the men stood and spoke in a similar manner, and just about as many women did as well. Somewhere during the night a consensus was reached, the voting not one of raising hands but one of acceptance that it was as it should be. An old, old man stood to speak. His hair was long and gray, braided, but still down to his waist. His face was deeply wrinkled, he still had all of his teeth and they shone a bright white against his dark and leathery skin. Jen whispered to me that this man was Big Bear, a cherished medicine man of great wisdom and deep spirituality, and that his speech would end the night and put a formality on my adoption by the tribe. He spoke barely above a whisper, and yet that soft, soft voice of his carried to all ears better than had any speaker's before him. There was power in this man; no one who listened could have thought otherwise.

"We have looked into this young warrior's heart,

and found it true. Little Giant Killer is a member of our tribe, and brings honor to us all."

Then he turned and looked into my eyes like no one else ever had before. I felt that he was seeing me, the true me deep inside, and at the same time seeing through me, to something beyond me, something that wasn't there for anyone else to see. It gave me goose bumps, sending a chill straight down my spine.

"Little Giant Killer, you are on a quest that will bring you many troubles. You will be in danger, grave danger, many times. Only by keeping your heart as true as it is now will you survive. Your journey will be interrupted by a quest that has to be completed before you can return to tracking the evil one. Guard your heart against all evil, trust your inner voice, keep your spirit true. You will be tested many times, but by staying true to our ways, those ways that are also yours, you may return to a life of peace and live to an old age surrounded by many that love and honor you."

I left the next morning, with many regrets and after a long and drawn out farewell from the villagers. In other circumstances I would have gladly accepted their offer to stay and live among them, become one of them. But I also knew that in other circumstances I would never have met them, that thinking otherwise was a pipe dream, and that staying was impossible.

Two weeks later I found a pair of puppies wandering miles from anywhere, I had no idea how they'd gotten way out where they were. About six months old from their teeth I'd say, maybe mastiff blood. They still had those needle sharp milk teeth as I found out. They wanted to be with a human, I could tell, so they'd been around at least one before. But boy were they skittish. I finally got one to take a piece of meat from my hand – he did it a bit vigorously, he was pretty scared and all, drew a little blood, nothing bad. I worked with them for a couple of hours before I rode off. At first they stayed where they were, but when I was almost out of sight they came loping up behind me. Already big dogs, they were going to grow into real beasts, based on the size of their huge, young paws. I dropped a piece of meat behind me now and then for them.

That night I took a chance and camped with a fire. The pups stayed back from the fire, but the draw of the meat kept them close enough. Next morning when I woke up, one was sleeping on either side of me. We ate breakfast and traveled on. Now they roamed around me and the horse in a big circle, always keeping me in sight, although often from a long distance.

By lunch time we were best friends. They sat right next to me, eagerly taking the bits of cold fried bacon I gave them, but far more gently. I found as much comfort in their company as they apparently found in mine. I slept better at night knowing they'd awaken me if there was trouble. I also had to bathe them every chance I got for they loved to roll in dead things, the stench staying in their fur. Thankfully they enjoyed being washed. I used Yucca root for soap.

It's been a year now – I passed my fifteenth birthday sometime back. My search for the killer has stretched out longer than I had thought it would. I'd thought I would catch up to him quick enough. But the truth is that the man making tracks can travel faster than the one slowly finding and following them.

I've lost and found the trail a number of times. I've been following a thread of his trail – a few whispers here and there, some rumors – until I lose it, and then I search until I find it again. I'll go on until I find him. I've had a few minor run-ins with some bad folks and come out okay so far, and I'm not as timid as I was when I started on this journey. Sometimes I worry that I'll turn mean myself, so I make it a point of personal honor to always be honest and friendly to everyone, until they prove I need to stop the friendly part. The honest part doesn't change with anyone. Trouble is that I'm finding it easier to be less friendly with each encounter of the bad sort. Still, I haven't had to kill anyone yet, but I have broken a bone or two, now and then.

I've grown quite a bit in the past year, gotten taller and broader in the shoulders. There's no fat on me because I am always on the move, the only time I rest is when I sleep. I've still got some growing yet to do, I believe but I'm over six feet already and I'd guess close to two-hundred pounds; and though I look thin, I'm as strong as anyone I've come across at my age, and stronger than a lot of grown men. My reflexes have steadily improved, I can move quick as a cat when I need to, and that has been damn handy on more than a few occasions.

The dogs – Zeke and Jake – are full grown now, well-behaved, and follow orders to a "T". They are huge, each weighing a solid one-hundred pounds and more of muscle. They're all black with black eyes and scary as hell looking – I'm pretty sure they're part wolf, and part something big like a Great Dane or Mastiff. They are, in fact, scary as hell if they don't take a shine to you. They've kept me out of several scrapes just by their presence, not a lot of men want to take on the three of us. But some do and on two occasions the dogs pitched into a fight I was in and their help was more than welcome. They're excellent trackers too. If I ever get close enough to the killer for them to get his scent it will be a lock to find him.

I'm in Idaho and it is a frigid winter. I stopped in a town and bought a half dozen Hudson Bay style blankets. These small towns all seem to look alike. They are the towns left over from before the solar storm that wiped out civilization back when my great, great, great grandfather Adrian Hunter was alive. Mostly they follow the same pattern – a main street with brick buildings on either side, old glass still in some, but most of the windows boarded over for lack of glass. The wooden buildings have all cratered in on themselves and are just piles of long forgotten memories. Brick still holds up pretty well. Hitching posts in front of the active stores and saloons because most folks ride horses. The asphalt and concrete of the streets have pretty much disappeared into small pieces of material, kind of like large gravel. At night you'd be hard pressed to make out more than a dim light streaming out through a cracked wall panel or the occasional dusty glass window. A lot of these towns I come across are ghost towns, others have only a half dozen or so people living in them.

Every now and then I'll find one that has a decent-sized population, but the smaller towns are more common. There are occasional strings of towns that are fairly well populated, generally in areas where there are a lot of farmers and farms. Sort of like back home, pockets of settled country. Surprisingly there is a good deal of trade across the country, mostly supplied by freighters with large wagons pulled by teams of six or more horses or mules. These freighters are a tough bunch. No one with any sense messes with freighters, as they generally travel in convoys of ten or more wagons, and every man of them is armed to the teeth and ready to fight. They still get hit by the occasional band of desperate raiders; mostly it turns out bad for the raiders.

Those thick wool blankets I mentioned are ideal for this weather. I made myself a greatcoat out of two of them, sewed double-thick, and I stayed tolerably warm, but not toasty, inside. When I had finished making my coat I made a coat for my horse. He looks sort of like the old drawings of armored horses in it. The coat fastens over his chest and a separate piece goes over his neck and head, with eye and ear holes. I figured it would help him stay warm, and it has. I take it off every day and brush him down and let him get a couple of hours of fresh air. At first I had some trouble getting the coat on him, but once he figured out how warm it kept him he stood docile as I put it on.

The dogs went out hunting this morning as I ate my breakfast over a small campfire. I've a need for warmth in the mornings, and with the dogs around feel a little safer about building one. Jake and Zeke mostly feed themselves; I just give them "treats." They are excellent hunters and are sometimes gone for several hours. They always find me though, and bless them, they'll often bring me a rabbit or other food they've killed. I started training them on how to track a specific person some time back. They are smart and learned the rules quickly – no barking, and no running ahead out of my sight. If the time comes, I don't want them to give it away that we are on his trail, and I don't want them shot by getting there too soon.

Eighty two years ago the earth was shattered. A dense cloud of large meteors collided with our planet and it rained bus size and larger stones for three days. Civilization is a fragile thing to the universe, and nearly half the population died within a month, mostly from starvation. The dust that was kicked up into the atmosphere blocked much of the sun's energy and years of winter followed, and many more died. Two successive blows, the sun storm and the meteor storm, left the nation a broken and shattered thing. We're coming back maybe, little by little, but there's no particular law other than what a man creates around him, and that almost always requires force or the credible threat of force.

The giants started showing up a generation or two after the hell storm. Some speculate that they rode down on the meteors, but that's just crazy talk. More likely a nuclear power plant was hit and the wide-spread radioactive fallout caused a mutation of some kind. More logical a theory perhaps, but just as unproven. Fact is no one really knows. These monsters are huge, and wear armor so they come from some place and that place has some kind of organization about it. There's lots of speculation as to where they come from, but no one that I've met knows where that is.

The years since the impact winter have warmed up some, although the winters are bitterly harsh. This winter had been no exception. The smart people, the survivors, tend to be smart people, stock up with plenty of food and fire wood and hole up all winter. But I couldn't take that kind of time – I didn't think my parent's killer would hole up, and if he did, I might gain precious time on him. So I pressed on, slowly, through the deep snow.

I made camp atop a ridge, where the wind had kept the snow from getting deep. This was wild and rocky country, on the edge of mountains. It was beautiful land, even covered in snow as it was. The wind was light most days and hardly any blew that night. During the night, after the fire had died down we were attacked by a pack of wolves.

Had it not been for the dogs warning me, and the bright moon and snow making the wolves visible, I wouldn't have survived. It was a close thing as it was. The dogs woke me up with frantic deep barking. I came up with my gun in hand, suddenly and acutely alert, just as the pack pressed in. It was a wild few moments, with Jake and Zeke each locked in separate mortal combats. They had taken on the first two, giving me a half second to pick off the third wolf as it gathered for its attack.

I killed four wolves, all told, and Jake and Zeke accounted for their two as well. The wolf pack reconsidered us as meals and fled, the entire snarling battle lasting only a minute. I built the fire back up high and spent the night skinning the dead wolves. The hides would make good trade items in the next town I came to and there wasn't going to be any more sleep for me that night anyway. Before skinning the wolves I tended to the dogs' wounds, sewing them up with hair from my horse's tail. They'd gotten off light, with few gashes, and would be okay for travel by the next morning. It showed how big and tough Jake and Zeke are, that they can take on and kill wolves with little damage to themselves.

I came to a medium size town the next day and rode down the main street. It looked like all the other towns I'd seen along the way. Hitching rails and horse troughs in front of a general store and saloon. I was bone tired and hadn't felt warm in forever. I stabled my horse at the local livery, then waded through snow to the saloon. Jake and Zeke came in with me and got some stares but no one said anything about them being in there. They lay down under the table as I sat.

To most folks it probably felt bitter cold inside the saloon, in spite of the sheet metal stove in the corner that was glowing cherry red with heat. The few patrons all had their coats on.

To me it felt like a blast furnace of heat inside and I stripped down to my shirt, basking in the warmth. I don't drink, but saloons are usually the best place to get information quickly; drinking men like to talk and the man I was after always went to the saloons when he was in town. I have found that many saloons also have food available. So once I was thoroughly thawed-out, I went up to the bar. The bartender looked at me suspiciously because I look my age. He appeared ready to refuse me service. It's a common occurrence, and I've learned how to deal with it.

Before he could order me out, I said "I'd take hot coffee and hot food, if you have any, and I can pay, and some meat scraps for the dogs."

His face relaxed and he replied, "Got all three. Coffee's fresh and we have stew in the back and some scrap meat and fat. You really got money young man?"

I placed one eighth of one of Pa's gold coins on the counter and he smiled. "First gold I've seen in a month. Have a seat and I'll fetch the food." That's the trick right there, don't ask for liquor and show the gold, but show it carefully. It dispenses with the age question every time. He poured a large mug full of coffee and brought it to my table, disappeared through a door behind the bar and reappeared seconds later with a bowl with steam rising from the top, a chunk of bread and a spoon, and a platter of raw meat pieces.

I tore into that stew and it was good, real good. Tossed the scraps to the dogs from time to time as I ate. I sopped up the last of the stew with the remainder of the bread and then settled back to sip the coffee. It was still hot. I had scarfed the food down in that much of a rush after the first bite. I was full, warm, and comfortable for the first time in weeks. Jake and Zeke were pretending to sleep, but I knew better. They were a comfort in places like this. Most any normal man would think long and hard about messing with me with these two huge beasts beside me

Business was slow and the bartender sat down at my table with his own mug of coffee and said "Son, you must have been out there for a long time to get here. We're a long way from anywhere even in good weather. What's your story?"

"I'm hunting a man that killed my Ma and Pa. Shot them down like dogs to steal a sack of gold coins." Reaching into my pocket I pulled out one of the coins. "Like this. I been on his trail over a year now, but seem to be losing it." I'd learned not to give out my name because unfortunately the giant killing story had traveled far and wide and it just made for complications I don't want.

"You're still on it," He replied. He picked the coin up off the table and looked at it closely, seeming to recognize it. "About six weeks ago, just after the first snow in fact. He come through here and stayed a couple days, got into a gunfight right over there at the bar with another fella and killed him. Let me warn you if you don't already know, he's damn fast with a gun, damn fast. And he don't hesitate to use it none neither."

"Did you see which way he rode out"

"The whole dang town saw which way he rode out. He was in the saddle and spurring his horse east before the gun shots had hardly finished echoing.

The sheriff took off after him, but the wind blew the tracks out fast and the sheriff's heart wasn't really in it anyway. Rumor has it he was spotted in Jared, about a hundred miles on east of here a couple weeks later, so he wasn't traveling all that fast."

I sat there thinking about this for a moment. A new customer came in and the bartender stood up, handed me the coin back. "I owe you plenty of change for that bit of gold son. I'll bring it to you directly.

I replied. "You've been a help, just keep it. Before you go, is there a gun smith in this town?"

"Not a full time professional one." He replied. "But old man Wurther takes care of most broken guns round here. He's got the general store down the street." He went back behind the bar and started talking to the new customer, obviously old friends from the bantering tone of their conversation.

I finished my coffee, shrugged into my coat, and followed the sidewalk to the general store, Zeke in front of me and Jake following. They often took those positions. Inside the store was nice and warm, too. It was a plain stock store, not much beyond the essentials on display. An old man was puttering around in the back and hollered out that he'd be with me in a second.

When he came out I was a bit surprised, but didn't show it. He looked like a dwarf in a white apron. A round and red face, white beard, and big hands, not an inch over four and a half foot tall. "Are you Mr. Wurther?" I asked.

"Yes sir, that I am. I see that my fame has preceded me. What can I do you for?"

"I hear you do some gunsmithing?"

"That I do sonny, that I do. What kind of gunsmithing you got in mind?"

I replied, "To tell you the truth sir I'd prefer to do my own work if I could rent your tools and bench for half a day or so?"

"Well now, that is an unusual request. I'd not mind but I don't want any of my tools misused. Some are fairly delicate and hard to replace."

"Mister Wurther my Pa taught me better than to misuse tools. I'll pay for any I damage though, if that makes you feel better about it." I showed him the same gold coin I'd shown the bartender.

"Ah!" His eyes fairly glowed at the sight of the gold. "That'd be fine then, just fine." He pointed to a closed door in the back and said "Just go through there and you'll find my work bench."

"You mind if my pups keep me company?"

"If those are pups I'm six feet tall." He chuckled. "Long as they behave themselves they're welcome."

He had a good bench, good tools, and a good strong light. I unloaded the cylinders and disassembled the pistol. Half a day was a bad guess. I should have known it would be, because once I start on a project like that I get lost in the work and time has no meaning. I was still working away when the old man came back and said "Son, I'm closing the store. You'll have to finish that in the morning. You got a place to stay the night? We don't have a hotel, you know."

I looked up from the piece I was working on and

blinked. "No sir, I hadn't given it any thought just yet. What do you recommend?"

"Well most travelers sleep in the livery stable, but its damn cold out there. I'll lend you the extra room in my house if you're of a mind to accept – and before you ask, yes the dogs, too. I like dogs, had some of my own over the years."

I accepted. I went to the livery stable and gathered up the wolf hides and brought them back to the store.

"If these have any value to you I'll trade them for the lodging."

"Sure, I can sell those, even green like that. Folks like to make coats of them." When we got to his house, he asked, "You hungry? Hell what am I saying? A boy your age is always hungry. I'll throw on some extra for you."

He was right, I am always hungry and his cooking was just fine, plain but fine. I slept hard that night and so did Jake and Zeke. Two good meals that close together and me being tired from the trail, all three of us piled onto a nice soft warm bed and we were fair-to-knackered to start with. It seemed I'd barely closed my eyes when I was startled awake by a knocking on the bedroom door. Light was just filtering in through the window. "You get up when you're ready. I left some biscuits and the coffee on the stove. Lock the door when you come out." I heard footsteps across the floor, then the sound of the front door opening and closing.

I was anxious to get back to work on my pistol, but not so anxious that I didn't eat the biscuits or drink the coffee. I gave each dog a biscuit, they loved them. When I returned to the store the old man gave me a broad smile. "Wish I could sleep the way you do, but age and aches keep an old man tossing and turning all night."

I thanked him for the hospitality of his home then went back to work on my pistol. About noon the old man popped into the workroom with two sandwiches, two large hunks of raw meat for the dogs, and more coffee. "Take a lunch break son, eat your sandwich and tell me what you're doing to that fine old pistol."

In between bites I explained. "I'm trailing a man that robbed and killed my parents. He was here about six weeks ago and shot a man in the saloon. The bartender said he was real fast with a gun. So I got to thinking I might need more of an edge when I find him. I enlarged the trigger guard and thinned it down on the sides so I won't fumble around getting my finger inside it if I'm in a hurry, and it'll work better for me if I'm wearing gloves, too. Then I filed off the front sight – don't use it anyway – and gently filed down the top side of the barrel so that its slightly tapered; should be faster coming out of the holster that way. I've adjusted the double action so that it takes minimal pull to fire and I'm polishing all the moving parts so that there is almost no friction. Last I'll cut down the front of the holster a bit so the barrel can come out just that much faster. What do you think?"

"I think you're a smart boy on a fool's mission. But if someone gunned down my folks I'd do the same as you, so I won't waste energy trying to argue you out of it. You any good with that gun?"

I replied as honestly as I could, "Fair. I've been practicing when I can. I can draw pretty good and I almost always hit what I'm aiming at, as long as it's within the gun's accuracy range, which really isn't all that much, fifty feet maybe."

"Fifty feet is about right. A short barrel doesn't garner much accuracy, never has, never will. But for up close fighting you can't beat it. You get finished and I'll show you a thing or two might help," he said cryptically. He finished his sandwich and coffee and returned to the front of the shop. I continued my work, taking my time and finished up just before he closed up again.

"Come on son, I've got a little shooting range out back." He locked the front door from the inside this time and we went out the back. There was nothing but trees behind the store and some targets set up at various distances. "Okay now, strap that rig on and shoot that forty-foot target. Draw as fast as you can without shooting your foot, and fire as fast as you can."

"I might need to shoot a few rounds to get the feel after all that work," I replied.

"You don't get no warm-ups or do-overs in a gunfight, son. Just draw and fire as though your life depended on it. I want to see what I'm working with here."

So I faced the target then drew and fired in one smooth motion, hitting the target just left of the bulls-eye.

The old man rubbed his chin for a few seconds then said, "That sucked."

I was a little taken aback. I had drawn and fired

as well as I ever had in practice, better than most times. The newly polished parts, the cut-down on the holster, and the now-missing sight blade had made it come clean of the holster and fire as smooth as butter, and I had nearly hit the bulls-eye. "I thought it was pretty decent, Mr. Wurther." I said defensively.

"Son, I was in the bar when that man you're hunting shot that fella, and you're not ready to take him on. Not yet. But you can be if you'll listen to me and practice hard for a few weeks. Right now he'd have you before you pulled the trigger. You've got to reduce your draw and fire time by half to beat him good – beat him by enough he won't get a shot off at you, too, that is."

And so three long days of intensive coaching followed. Everything was dry-fire for the first two days. He would correct something I was doing, tell me to work on it, and then go back in the store. After a while he'd come out and check my progress, make more corrections, and leave again. At first my arm was getting tired, but as his corrections took hold and I learned a new way to draw and fire, I found my arm wasn't getting at all tired, telling me that I had been wasting a lot of energy before, wasting motion.

Before we had gotten started I asked, "How do you know enough about fast draw shooting to teach me to do it better? No offense Mr. Wurther, but I don't want to learn mistakes from someone I barely know."

The old man laughed hard at that question. When he finally caught his breath he said, "Son, the reason I'm taking time with you is just because you ask questions like that. You're smart, and you're direct, and yet you're polite about asking a hard question of a man that says he's trying to do you a favor. And most of all you're right to ask. I like you son, you've got a good mind and a good temper. To answer your very direct question, I used to be in a traveling circus. You may have noticed that I'm a bit short. But of course you're too polite to say so." He grinned at my guilty look.

"This was a small circus, no more than ten of us all together. We traveled from town to town and barely made enough to live on. One of the acts in the circus was a real tall man that was faster than you can believe with a pistol, and deadly accurate. He could draw, fire three times at an ace of spades sixty feet away, then reholster, and I swear you could not see it happen. You'd swear you only heard one shot at that, but there would be three holes touching the center ace. Anyway that was his act. Well, times got even slower than before, and the circus owner thought it might improve the take to have a great tall man and a dwarf in a gun battle as one of the acts.

"I had never shot a gun and didn't see how it would work but that pistolero started teaching me, and me not having any bad habits to unlearn, I learned pretty quick. We fought it out for about three years in the center stage, using red chalk bullets and thick leather breast plates. I got faster and faster, but never had a shade on that man. Then I had a chance to buy this store with my savings and I've been here ever since. Here let me show you."

40

He came back out of the store with a fancy pistol rig decorated with large bright silver Conchos, strapped it on, squared up with the target and proceeded to draw and shoot far faster than I had. "Now you know what I can teach you, and I've slowed down some from lack of practice." He smiled and returned to the store. I stared at the closed door for a long time, then started doing everything he taught me. I was convinced.

He taught me a lot of things, but the most powerful was to shoot from just above the holster. I had been drawing, then raising my arm out in front of me before pulling the trigger. He taught me how to be more accurate and much faster by grabbing the gun, raising it just enough to clear the holster, bend my wrist up and fire.

When I had that down he showed me to start pulling the trigger as soon as I grabbed the gun handle. That way the gun was already cocked and would fire as I straightened my wrist. Dangerous as hell with a loaded gun, but it shaved mili-seconds off the clock. After three days he said I had it down, but that I would need to practice several hours every day to beat it into my muscle memory so that when the time came I wouldn't have to think, just do.

He also told me that to survive a gun fight it was best to shoot your opponent in the head. "How many deer have you shot right through the heart and it still ran a hundred yards? Men are like deer that way, shoot one in the heart and he can still shoot back for a few seconds, and knowing you killed him he will be motivated to. The only sure way is a head shot. But the head is a hard target to hit, so you have to be close enough that you can't miss, which means even an average shooter won't miss your chest either. So you have to be able to do two things, shoot before he does, and shoot him in the head. Shoot a man in the chest and he has a better than average chance of living long enough to shoot you, too. Shoot him in the head and he'll drop straight down."

My advanced class from Mr. Wurther was drawing and shooting at an old civilization rubber ball half the size of a man's head. The ball was suspended from a piece of rope and I had to learn to draw and hit it while the ball was swinging. Mr. Wurther was right, I had to be within thirty feet to be confident with that shot. I carried the ball with me when I left, and practiced with it until it was in shreds. Then made one of leather. Eventually I lost count of how many I made.

Mr. Wurther said that in time I'd find my "sweet spot – the distance that I had the best accuracy on a moving head shot, and they're always moving. "Too close is no better than too far," he told me. "You'll find it naturally. That's the distance you need to be at in a face-to-face, quick-draw shoot out. You'll find it. Just remember it and use it."

Months passed quickly as I followed the sightings of the man I had sworn to kill. I was gaining on him again, but slowly. He had holed-up in a small town some way east for a month and I had left after the quick draw lessons. It was a fond parting, Mr. Wurther was truly a good man to have for a friend.

I left a decent-sized pile of gold pieces where he'd find them after I was gone. I knew he would never have accepted them, and they were enough he could retire on if he wanted to, but I suspect the store was more than a source of income to him and that he would keep running it. Now he would be financially secure in his old age. It was far less than I owed him.

I practiced hard every day with the gun, often for hours at a time. Mostly dry fire, as ammunition wasn't all that easy to come by and if I shot every time I drew I'd be out of bullets in a day. But I did practice with live rounds now and then to make sure I was hitting what I wanted to hit. I also picked up a portable reloading kit. By experimentation I found just the right charge for the bullets and that improved my accuracy quite a bit. Little by little I became extremely fast and deadly accurate. I felt ready to take on my nemesis when I finally found him.

I soon had a chance to learn how fast I was. I was riding a high lonely trail through a rocky area. The trail narrowed to go between large boulders that had gnarly little cedars growing out of the cracks and crevices. As I entered the pass, I saw a flash of brown blur rocketing down at me. No thought was involved, there wasn't time for thought. Blurred flash of brown and then my gun exploding three times. The mountain lion's body hit me as it fell, but it was dead when it got to me. Two bullets in the head and one in the throat, and all in far less than a second. When the horse stopped bucking and carrying on I rode back and skinned the cougar, keeping the hide, the skull and the claws. They would make good trade items, and trade items were less conspicuous than gold. I have to admit to feeling a bit cocky about it, but that cockiness would soon come face to face with reality, and disappear again.

It was in another small town saloon where I had stopped to inquire. The bartender had objected to the dogs and so I'd left them outside by my horse. Back inside a belligerent man saw that I was wearing a pistol and decided that he could kill me, me being so young-looking and all. He started with the usual stuff, bumping me and accusing me of bumping him, calling me names, and working himself into a lather. Normally I would have apologized nicely for bumping into him, even though I hadn't, but instead I just stared at him without speaking, daring him more or less. That was the cockiness coming out in me.

We were facing each other and he took three steps back and set himself. I watched his gun hand, not his face, another tip from Mr. Wurther. His hand blurred down to his pistol. Before he cleared the holster I had mine out and, and having plenty of time, I straightened my arm out in front of me so that he could see it clearly. I've heard-tell of the blood leaving a man's face white as snow, this time I saw it happen. I didn't fire of course, no need to. By ordinary standards he was fast and had a reputation for being fast. He found out that he wasn't as fast as he thought he was, and maybe it changed his life, I don't know. I came that close to killing him.

Had it happened before the mountain lion incident I'd have found a way out of the confrontation. I didn't like that feeling in me, that sureness, that cockiness. That's what gets men killed. It was a different lesson for the both of us, but we both learned something hard about ourselves.

I don't want a reputation as a fast gun, I only want to kill one man. When the back slapping part by the saloon's patrons commenced someone asked my name and I didn't answer. Someone else asked where I was from and I lied for the first time in a long, long time and said "Itasca Texas." I heard "Itasca Kid" murmured through the crowd. I got out of town pretty quick after that, as I didn't need any more wannabe gunslingers coming at me. From time to time I've heard people talk of the "Itasca Kid" in my travels, but no one so far seems to have figured out it was me. I aim to keep it that way.

Pa was great with steam engines and steam driven devices and he taught me everything I know about it. I know a lot more about it than anyone I've come across since, but it's still not a scratch on what Pa knew. There are times when it comes in handy to fix a steam machine for folks. I eventually started telling people that I'm a steam mechanic when I come into a new town. It's largely a barter economy pretty much everywhere I've traveled, and certain skills are in high demand. Being able to repair steam engines is more valuable than the gold I carry – and I always enjoy the work. Give me the run of a good blacksmith shop and I can make almost any part needed. Not to mention, I've gotten lots in return for working on machinery. Information, ammunition, food, lodging, whatever I need I've gotten in exchange for a little steam work. I've been offered many a full time job. Truth is, I could set up my own factory, train good workers, then build and repair steam engines and become wealthy. But I'm on a mission. Besides, I am already rich, back home, so I'm not tempted.

This skill with steam came in handy a lot of times, but possibly one of the most valuable was in a place called Watson. I'd ridden into town, stabled my horse, and told the livery man that I was a steam mechanic and could use a spot of work if he knew of anyone with a need. He did.

I walked over to the local power plant, one of many like it that had sprung up in the larger cities to furnish electricity to local businesses and some of the wealthy residences. Mr. Jotter owned the plant and had a steam engine down, cutting his sales in half, and he was desperate. His mechanic had died a week before and there was no one in town he could turn to. He was a businessman, not a mechanic. He would have paid me a fortune, but a fortune I didn't need. What I wanted was information.

"No sir, I don't want to be paid in gold or any other form of money. What I need is information." I explained who I was after, and why. "If you'll ask everyone in town that might know something about him, I'll fix your power plant."

"But, what if no one knows anything? What do I do then?"

"Why just tell me that. All I ask is you put a solid effort into it. I'll fix the machine just the same. In fact I'll fix it while you're asking around."

He shook my hand and was out the door before I could change my mind, not believing his good luck.

I grinned and went over to the big old steam engine and began several tests on it. It didn't take long to figure out that a bearing had frozen up. It took me two days to tear it down, pull the bearing and make another one like it, then put it back together again and gin her back up. She ran sweet as could be.

When I was done I told Mr. Jotter what had been wrong, what I had done, and that while I had it apart I'd checked it all out thoroughly and fixed a few other things that were wearing down. "Treat it right and it's good for many years."

Then I got my payoff. Mr. Jotter had taken his mission to heart; the man would have made a great detective. He'd poked and pried and listened and cajoled for two straight days and had found that my parent's killer had indeed been in town for a bit over a week about two months past. Better than all that, he'd found one man that said the killer had told him he was heading north to Bisam, a town a couple of hundred miles away. He also found out that he called himself Oscar. Had it not been for that seized bearing I would have lost the trail right there because I figured he was still heading east. I was on the trail again that day.

———◆———

My time is divided between being alone in the wilderness and socializing with folks in the towns I visit. I'm comfortable in both cases, but lately I've been thinking about my future and whether or not a family will be in it. I guess in the long run I don't want to live alone after I go back home. It's a good ranch, but it's in a lonely place, and the thought of years of solitude held little appeal. It's odd that when you really need something, it can just appear, even though you might not recognize it at the time. When I needed a teacher, Mr. Wurther was just right there for instance. When I needed a fresh start on the trail, that broken steam engine belonging to a man that knew everyone in town was right there.

I was way out in the sticks, far between small towns when I stopped to camp near a burned-out cabin for the night. It was a small homestead that'd been deserted. There were two graves nearby, still carefully tended though and that made me wonder a bit about who's been tending them. I built a fire and had bacon frying while I sat comfortably against an old tree. The dogs lie down near me, but they never seem to fully sleep. It's a great comfort knowing that no one is going to sneak up on me. The dogs always let me know when someone is near. They have a good sense of who is dangerous, too. This time their low, deep rumbling growl that I could barely hear let me know someone was near, but that they weren't too concerned. So I sat and waited. And waited. And nearly fell asleep while waiting. Maybe it was someone just passing by and I'd never see him.

Then Zeke raised his head and looked off in the distance, and I knew I was about to have company for sure. Sure enough a little boy of maybe ten years slowly walked up towards the fire. When he got close he said "Mister, I sure hate to bother you, but do you have any food you can spare?"

I didn't; I don't carry a large amount of food with me, but I said "Sure." I got up and cut off half the bacon I had left and handed it to him. "Want me to cook it for you?"

"Thank you sir, but I got a fire over yonder." He was holding that bacon like it was the last piece on earth, gripped tightly in both hands. "Thank you again, Mister." He turned and fled into the darkness. Now I'm no crusader or anything but letting a young boy, obviously half-starved, just run away into the dark like that didn't set right with me. Almost anything could happen to that kid, and not one bit of it would be good. I sat there pondering on what to do for a few minutes, then I had an idea. I told the dogs, "Go fetch that boy back here." Like dark lightning streaks they were off. I knew they wouldn't hurt him, they'd just herd him back like the lost lamb he was – or that I thought he was. I waited. And waited. And wondered what in the world was taking so long. Maybe the boy had gone up a tree and I'd have to go find him when the sun came up.

A full two hours later, as measured by the swing of the stars, I heard a soft bark, then another and another. I knew it was the dogs herding the boy back to me. I was wrong. They were herding a whole flock of children.

Six kids came slowly into the firelight. They ranged in size from a girl that looked near my age down to a little boy she was carrying, and the other four looked about a year apart in age from each other. All had dark hair and blue eyes, small noses – and at the moment, very unhappy expressions. Definitely siblings, each and every one of them, those apples had fallen straight down from the family tree. If I was to guess I'd say the oldest girl was about fifteen and the youngest maybe four.

I groaned as they stood silently, staring at me with open hostility. For someone used to being alone, that was a lot of unhappy eyes staring at me. "Zeke, Jake, settle down," I said quietly. The dogs immediately came from behind the kids and lay down on either side of where I was still sitting. The children were frightened enough already, and standing up may have had a hostile tone to it, so I remained sitting where I was, lower than they were. Sometimes the little things help a lot.

"Just what the hell do you think you're doing siccing those horrid monsters on us?" This from the oldest girl. She wasn't too happy with me, I noticed that right off, being the observant type that I am.

"I'm sorry." I replied as gently and sincerely as I could. "I didn't know you were out there; just the one boy, and I wanted to make sure he was all right."

"Scaring the hell out of Bert in the dark with these giant black dogs is your way of making sure he's all right?" she replied with scorn. She thought she was in a bad spot, but she sure wasn't showing any sign of backing down. I admired her courage, but kept that to myself.

"Yes, it was. Jake and Zeke wouldn't hurt him for the world, and they would be able to find him, something I couldn't do in the dark. Look, I was trying to be helpful. You all look like you could use a good meal. I've enough food to make one meal for each of you, if you're interested."

The girl looked at me for a long time. I could see some of the tension leave her shoulders and her face softened a fraction. Food appeared to be their weak spot. She was sure a pretty girl, too. "You're a surprise. I expected to find some gnarly old bearded man looking to do us harm, and find a boy my age instead. A meal for the kids would be wonderful. Thank you." I didn't miss the implication that she wouldn't be joining in the meal. Either she didn't intend to accept anything from me for herself, or she wanted the kids to have a bit more food, I wasn't sure which. Maybe both.

"It's my pleasure Miss. By the way, my friends call me Robert. What's your name?"

"I'm Anna, and these are Bert, Darla, Jim, Crane, and Jessie. We have a pretty good camp about a mile from here; it's a lot more comfortable than this. You want to join us over there? We also have pots and pans."

I stood up, stretched. A bit of alarm ran through her face again as I towered over her. I'd not traded the mountain lion skin after all, but instead had made a coat of it, decorated with the claws and teeth in prominent places. Big as I was, that coat still hung down to my knees, and I'd left the head on for a hood I could pull up over my own head when conditions called for it. I must have been a scary sight to her and the kids. I know I looked like a primitive wild man. "Let's go." I said and smiled.

They had built a lean-to big enough to keep all of them out of the main weather. It was open in front with a fire pit built of rocks stacked up high on the backside to reflect heat into the lean-to's open front. The camp was clean and neat. Fallen logs on either side of the fire provided places to sit. It looked to me

LLOYD TACKITT

that they had been here for quite a while. I figured the mystery of who had been tending those graves was solved.

I removed all of the food from my saddle bags and Anna quickly started it cooking as the children watched with wide-eyed anticipation. It was plain food, beans and bacon, but there were a couple of jars of peaches also. Anna seasoned the beans with a few pieces of fried bacon, put in some of the salt and pepper I had, and let them boil. Beans take a while to cook, so we had time to talk before eating.

"What's your story Anna? Why are you and your brothers and sisters camping out here in the wilderness?"

"You saw the burned house. That was ours, we lived there with our parents. The house caught fire late one night, about three months ago. Dad got all of us kids out safely but Mom was still inside. Dad went back in to get her. Neither one came back out. That was in the dead of winter but there was food in the root cellar. We hoped to make it to spring and then figure out what to do next. We ate the last of the food last week and have been living on rabbits and squirrels and a few fish since. Not eating a lot though."

I said, "I'm awful sorry to hear about your parents. I lost mine a little while ago too. Do you have any family you can go to? Any neighbors?"

"No Robert. No family at all; and the only neighbors we have I wouldn't trust as far as I could spit a rat." I noticed that she had called me Robert and that was as good as a handshake under the circumstances. I liked the way it sounded when she said it.

There was a long silence after that. The children moved around a bit and whispered to each other occasionally, but overall they were silently watching the food cook. They were near starving, and the time it was taking to get the food ready to eat must have seemed like an eternity to them.

"What about you Robert? What's your story?"

So I told it, and they listened without blinking. I told them how I came home to find Ma and Pa murdered, how I was hunting their killer. Told them how I found and trained the dogs and some of the funnier things I had seen along the way. Told them about the mountain lion, too, but not about the man in the bar as I was not particularly proud of that event. I stretched it out as long as I could to help keep their minds off their hunger. By the time I finished, the meal was ready, and had been for a good five minutes, but none of them had so much as glanced at the food while I talked. They weren't just starved for food, they were also starved for company and stories and news. My showing up, the dogs, the food; it must have seemed a remarkable day to them.

Anna went into the lean-to and came back with bowls and spoons. I lied to her and said "I'm not hungry, I ate just before you guys showed up." Well the eating part wasn't a lie, but I was always hungry. She gave me a funny look but didn't protest, just ladled out portions to each child according to size. I noticed she didn't take any for herself, but I kept quiet about it. None of the other kids noticed, or if they did they didn't say anything. I suspect she had been eating next to nothing for a while now, trying to take better care of the kids that way. I admired that.

The children ate with intensity, each focused only on their own bowl of food, eating the fried bacon with fingers. They chased every bean down and two of them even licked their bowls as best they could. It was heartbreaking to watch. Anna divided the peaches up for a desert, it was pitifully small portions and disappeared almost instantly. After the meal Anna got the kids into the lean-to and tucked each one in with a kiss.

Anna and I sat on opposite sides of the fire for most of an hour until it was clear from their breathing that the kids were all asleep. My mind was awhirl with what I was going to do next. One thought was clear, I couldn't just ride away in the morning and leave them out in the middle of nowhere to starve to death. The only other option was to take them with me to the next town and try to find some friendly people to take them in – and I knew that wasn't going to be an easy sell. Not many would welcome that many mouths to feed into their home; most folks were struggling as it was.

In years I wasn't much older than Anna, but in another way I was now the adult in the group. It was an unsettling feeling, yet it was appealing all the same. I had assumed a responsibility, assumed it freely and willingly, but it was a heavy weight on my still young shoulders. I didn't ask Anna if she would approve of me taking on this role, I sensed she had already willingly accepted it also. There was a lot said between us that wasn't said in words. I knew that she wanted what was best for her family, and right now that was through me and what I could do for the kids. It may seem a cold calculation to folks that live in comfort, but it is survival that counts when you're facing a slow death by starvation, at best. It's the way of the world, always has been, and I found no discordant note in it.

Anna yawned for the third time, then said "I'm going to bed now. Thank you so much for the food, Robert. I'm sorry we wiped out your supplies." She stood and then walked into the lean-to, settling down between the two youngest children.

I got up, called the dogs softly and went to my horse. I could see Anna looking at me as I saddled up and rode off. I could only imagine what she was thinking. Thinking that she had judged me as being someone to help, but seeing me ride off like that figuring she had been wrong.

The moon was full and there was enough light to do some close hunting. I rode off a couple of miles and found some likely looking country, and told the dogs to hunt. They streaked off and pretty soon I heard them yelp a few times. When hunting animals they were allowed to make enough noise that I could keep track of them. They had a deer on the run from the sound of it. I plotted an intercept course, rode to it, and waited. Deer have a comfort with their immediate territory and will circle and circle to stay within the area where they know every tree, every rock, every blade of grass. This one was no different.

Ahead of the dogs I heard the sound of a deer busting through brush. When I saw it I raised my rifle and shot, once. I gutted the deer on the spot feeding the heart and liver to the dogs, then dragged it over to a large tree limb, pulled it up off the ground with a rope then quickly skinned and quartered it. I packed it all up, then rode back to the camp and settled down in my bedroll for a couple of hours of sleep. Neither Anna or the kids woke up when I came back, I was that quiet about it.

Just before dawn I arose, stirred the fire and placed more wood on it, and then started carving deer steaks and frying them in the bacon grease left over from the night before. Let me tell you, when the smell of that cooking meat hit those sleeping kids, they woke right up. Anna woke up last. The look of relief on her face nearly made my heart burst. I made her take the first steak and she didn't refuse at all. We sat there gnawing on some fairly tough meat, but it was hot and juicy and wonderful. We had enough meat for two more meals.

As the kids took the dishes down to a creek to wash, I said, "Anna, take a seat, we've got some talking to do." She sat down on one of the logs and I did as well. "I've been pondering on this all night. I can't go off and leave you all here, you'll starve – or something even worse. If anything happened to you, something as simple as a broken leg, you'd all die. These kids are too small to take care of themselves. I just can't leave you or them like that."

Anna replied, "I thought you left last night and it scared me no end. It made me realize how badly we need help, but we have no place to go."

"I've got an idea about that. It will be hard and dangerous, but less dangerous than remaining here. First thing is we need to get to the next town."

They had their two old plow mules hobbled nearby. We went to fetch them and Anna said "I was going to slaughter one today to feed the kids." She said it in a matter-of-fact tone, but I heard the relief in her voice just the same. Back at the lean-to we packed a few dishes and pots and pans, and with two kids riding each mule and Anna and one other riding my horse, I began leading them out of the wilderness.

It took over six weeks to get to the next town. We couldn't go any faster than I walked. From time to time Anna would walk with me to stretch her legs. I made sure the kids stayed up on their mounts. I know it was uncomfortable for them after several hours, but that way none of them could wander off or step on a snake. It was just safer that way. We stopped early to camp every day so that I could go hunting and the kids could stretch out. There were a couple of stretches of two or three days when I didn't bring back any meat, and our bellies really gnawed at us. When I would come back with game the kids really lit up, and it always kindled a fire in me, but not nearly as big a fire as Anna caused with her smiles.

Anna and I talked a lot during those weeks. Long talks, deep talks. Talks about dreams of the future. The kind of talks young people falling in love make. In spite of our hardships we laughed a lot, and the kids laughed nearly all the time. About the only time they fell silent was when eating or sleeping. As a matter of fact I was in love of the kids from the first night. I slowly fell in love with Anna, and she with me, but a different kind of love from what I had for the kids. We were both young and hadn't either of us been around someone our own age much, and so even under the circumstances, it was a shy and awkward courtship.

Sometimes the travel was pleasant, but mostly it was just hard and boring. I'd worn out my boots and had made moccasins of green deer skin, double-soled as my feet were tender from having been protected by good boots. I wore those moccasins out and found to my surprise that Anna had made me another pair, doing it when I was off hunting then hiding them until she had another opportunity to work on them when I was gone. The ones she made were far more skillfully crated than my own had been – I'd just thrown them together quickly, and that's why they wore out so fast. These were well-made, sturdy, and fit me perfectly. She'd turned mine inside out while I was asleep one night and made a pattern based on the wear marks inside. They also came nearly to my knees and afforded a lot more protection against thorns and tearing brush, and they were handsome in a mountain-man kind of way. I was so pleased that I blushed and stammered when she offered them to me. I think she blushed near as much as I did; it was obvious that she was proud she could do something for me for a change.

We had a few minor problems along the way, mostly caused by predatory animals coming up close to look us over to see if a meal was in the offering, a meal being one of us or the horses and mules. I'd had to shoot a bear, which made a fine robe for Anna, and several wolves, which made fine coats for the kids. We didn't waste anything we didn't have to, but I have to tell you, wolf steak sucks, and we only tried it the once. It makes passable jerky, though.

By the time we got to a town, I knew we'd all look like feral people that had -never seen civilization. Looking at us made me think of the pictures of cave men I'd seen in books, all covered in fur and with long hair. But at least it was clean hair – we all bathed as often as we could. So I made up my mind that I'd buy clothes and bring them out to the kids before we went into town. We'd all be dressed in regular clothes when we entered a town. Otherwise we might get shot on sight. I had one change of regular clothes I always carried with me, but Anna and the kids had only the clothes they wore, or what was left of them, the rest had burned in the house.

We ran into one big trouble about a week before we reached the town. A group of three rough men rode up on us. They were big and dirty and bearded and rode rangy horses. And they were armed to the teeth. From the instant they saw Anna, it was clear what they had in mind. I figured someone was going to die right there – I just had to make sure it wasn't Anna or any of the kids. Or me if I could help it. So I immediately walked straight at them, putting myself between these three renegades and the kids. I walked straight at them in a non-threatening way, just acting a bit curious is all. When I reached my sweet spot, I stopped.

"You men had better turn around and ride hard while you're still breathing," I said in a loud but calm voice. I was calm too. Inside I felt like a block of ice. My vision had sharpened to a point where everything had hard edges and was crystal clear.

What I didn't need to see had faded from my sight. Jake and Zeke had moved around behind the men and were in tense crouches, ready for anything. The trees behind the men weren't visible to me any longer, just these three men from their gun belts up was all I could see, I was that focused.

I didn't miss a detail of the mounted men. I watched their filth-covered hands, black grime under the nails, closely. I'd heard that you could tell when a man would draw by a change in his eyes, and that might be true for some folk, but I knew I could tell when they drew by watching their hands, Mr. Wurther had explained that and I had experienced it myself. I saw their faces just as clearly, saw the dirty grease in their beards, their yellowed teeth when they spoke, the wickedness of their eyes. Yes, someone was going to die in the next few seconds, of that I had no doubt.

I was also aware that even if they rode off they'd just circle around and look for a chance to shoot me in the back. This needed to end here, but if they rode off I'd let them. I won't kill in cold blood – except for one man that is.

I didn't want it this way, didn't want this confrontation, it's just the way it played out, more a matter of chance than anything. There are times when we have to act against our better nature, forced into it by circumstance. This looked to be one of them. I knew I was going to have to kill them sooner or later, knew it in my bones, and I preferred sooner. But they had to make the first move and I felt pretty sure that's just what they'd do.

The leader, a man with two missing teeth, began

laughing after I stopped talking. When he calmed down a bit he said, "Little boy, you best turn tail and run, 'cause if you don't you'll be dead before you hit the ground. These girls belong to us now." The other two guffawed in a hard and predatory way.

"Mister," I said. "You've got no chance. I can put a bullet in all three of your heads before one of you can get a gun pointed in my general direction. Now all you got to do is call that bluff, if you're a mind to."

They were done with words, given that two of them immediately went for their pistols. They moved at the same time, quick vicious stabs of their hands towards their side arms. They were at a slight disadvantage being mounted; it's awkward to draw while sitting in the saddle. I know, I've practiced at it quite a bit. I was standing flat-footed on the ground and had no such problem. Knowing all this instinctively I took a bit of extra time drawing my pistol just to be sure that I nailed them. Even at that my hand flashed faster than their eyes could see and the three shots rang out as one continuous roar. Three head shots, clean and true. Just like shooting at the swinging ball. Not one shot did they fire. They were dead before they knew they were dead. About as good an end as they could have come to, given their evil natures.

"Thank you Mr. Wurther." I whispered to myself. What he'd taught me had made this child's play, and I knew it had saved all of our lives today.

I hadn't lied to them, hadn't bluffed them, had given them a chance to ride away. I'd told them what I could do and what I would do, and then I did it when they forced my hand. They'd had a choice, I hadn't. As their bodies hit the ground I felt nothing for them or for the act of killing them, it had been their decision to not believe me. I didn't feel any more for killing them than I had the wolves that had attacked me and the dogs that one night. We didn't bury them, that was too much work for such low-lifes. We did keep the horses and guns and what little food they had, and we rode on from there with a much better distribution of horses among us. I got to ride again, too, and I was mighty glad for it.

After the shooting, Anna and the kids stared at me silently, with great big eyes. They were awful quiet for a long time afterwards too. Eventually Anna said, in a shaky voice, "That was damn fine shooting, Robert. Damn fine." It was the only time I'd heard her curse. I just nodded, and with that we rode on.

That night, after the still mostly-silent children went to sleep around our campfire, Anna said "Robert, I thank you. You stood between us and those horrible men. God only knows what they would have done to us, but it's certain it would have been an unending horror. Our own deaths would have been better than letting them get their hands on us. Far better. Where in the world did you learn to shoot like that? I'm still in shock at how fast it all happened; and your hand, I didn't even see it move, and I only heard one shot." She was slowly shaking her head from side to side.

"Mr. Wurther, a fine man I met on the trail, took the time to teach me – and I thanked him for it today." So I told her about my lessons. While I was telling her, the thought occurred to me that I could teach Anna and the oldest boy Bert, and now we had the extra guns to work with. I began the next morning with the lessons.

Day by day, the two of them got faster and more accurate. I took it in little steps, so as not to overwhelm them, teaching safety first, then accuracy, then drawing and shooting accurately, working on speed last. They were apt learners, and having seen first-hand how important it was to be good with pistol work, they set to it with a will. Anna learned faster, being older than Bert, and was better than most men after a week. But Bert though, he had a knack for it, and as he grew older I knew he would get better and better, and that someday he'd be hell on wheels itself.

When we finally reached the town of Apex it was a disappointment. It had been a hard trip, too often a hungry trek, and we had been all alone in the world, depending on each other, getting to know each other. I was saddened that the trip was over. I changed clothes, rode in, bought clothes for Anna and the kids, and quickly returned. I didn't like leaving them alone. It only took a few hours to realize that there was no one in the town that would take them in for more than a couple of days. I was secretly glad about that, and Anna might have been also, although she didn't say so right out, but I could tell. She was in love with me, too, I was pretty sure, but we were both still awful shy about it. I think she was guarding herself against me leaving them, afraid of being abandoned. I couldn't blame her a bit. I hadn't yet explained the slowly growing plan that I had developed as we traveled.

After a huge feast for the family, as I had come to think of us, at the town's only restaurant – where we caused something of a stir what with the dogs and all – Anna and I got the kids settled in for the night at the hotel then we took a walk. Those kids fell smooth in love with those beds and sheets let me tell you, and were snuggled in tight in no time. We'd all had blessedly hot baths with real soap and I'd bought ,us all new clean clothes. We felt civilized for the first time since we'd met. I left the dogs in the room with the kids. The kids would be well protected while we were gone.

"Anna, I have a proposal for you." Her eyes startled at the word and she looked at me with a longing that near stopped my heart from beating. "I'm thinking that we are going to have to take different trails." I rushed on before the quick shadow of disappointment that flicked in her eyes could turn to despair. "But just for a while. I'm thinking that you and the kids can travel to my ranch in Texas. It's a long trip, but it should be a fairly safe trip, mostly by train and then through settled country. When you get there you can settle in. It's a good ranch and has a good garden spot and there are seeds in storage ready to plant. There's plenty of beef on the range that you can eat as well. The root cellar should still be full of canned goods and potatoes that my Ma put away. You'll have plenty of food, good shelter, and good neighbors. I'll tell you where to find enough gold to buy anything you need for years to come, if it comes to that, and I hope it won't. There is a fantastic library of books there, you can school the kids. There are worlds of education in that library, finer than they could get at any school, and the nearest school is too far away anyway." And then, for the first time, I then told her my full name, and saw recognition grow with delight across her face.

"The thing is that I can't go with you, I have to find my folk's murderer and put him down. As soon as I do I'll turn south and ride for Texas as hard as I can. I'm thinking that when I get back we can get married, if you'll have me." I blurted that last bit out and then stopped there, suddenly all out of words and blushing something awful. I was in mortal fear that she would say no. Facing those three bad men hadn't scared me, but this sure as hell did. This, well this terrified me. I had no idea what I'd do if she said no, but I knew my world would coming crashing down.

Anna grabbed me in a hard hug, and kissed me gently on the lips. Then she pulled back, suddenly blushing like crazy as well.

"I'll take that as a yes." I said in a choked voice. The long, mutually searching and reassuring kiss that followed stirred me deeper than I had known I could be stirred, and obviously had as strong of an impact on her. We sat down on a bench in front of the general store and talked the sun up. We wouldn't see each other for as long as it took me to complete my hunt and get back home, and we had a lot of talking to do to hold us until then. We held hands, sitting there side by side, and stopped to kiss each other often. The hours rolled by like seconds, and well before we were ready the town started to come to life.

The travel arrangements were vastly simplified by having gold to pay for it. First would be a week-long trip with a freight hauler who was returning with empty wagons to Boise, a true city and one of the few that remained so. From Boise they would travel by steam train all the way to Fort Worth, at least three weeks of travel and possibly more. There were very few steam trains to start with, and they broke down often – tracks were often damaged by giants and had to be repaired, and tickets were higher than a cat's back to boot.

In Fort Worth, Anna would buy a team and a wagon, stock up with food and clothes, and go to the ranch, holding a rifle all the way, just in case. A rifle is a far better defense than a pistol, you can shoot someone long before they get into pistol range, and rifle bullets hit a lot harder than pistol bullets. I drew a careful map and showed her where to stop each night along the way. I gave her letters of introduction to give to our three closest neighbors, and asked them to watch out for Anna and the kids as they could.

I drew another map to the location of one of the gold stashes, enough for her and the kids for a life time, and cautioned her about being too flagrant spending it, lest she draw unwanted attention. I made her memorize that map then burned it. I bought her and Bert new pistols and had concealed holsters made for each of them. I explained about not trusting strangers – unnecessarily of course – but still I had to do it. She just smiled fondly at me as I mother-henned her, but didn't protest that I was telling her the obvious. We sold the mules, and they fetched a good price as matched mules were a thing of some value, and I gave her enough gold coins to cover the trip's expenses three times over, just to be sure.

When it came time to part it was the second saddest day of my life. The children cried something awful and Anna and I had tears as well. But we both knew that I could never settle down until I had brought death to the man I hated.

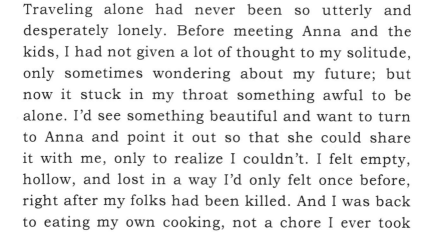

Traveling alone had never been so utterly and desperately lonely. Before meeting Anna and the kids, I had not given a lot of thought to my solitude, only sometimes wondering about my future; but now it stuck in my throat something awful to be alone. I'd see something beautiful and want to turn to Anna and point it out so that she could share it with me, only to realize I couldn't. I felt empty, hollow, and lost in a way I'd only felt once before, right after my folks had been killed. And I was back to eating my own cooking, not a chore I ever took much pains with.

I had lost a lot of time on the trail with Anna and the kids, and Oscar was well ahead of me now. The horses we'd gotten from the renegades weren't in very good condition, so I'd sold them and then bought a second riding horse and a pack horse so that I could carry enough food to not need to hunt so often, so I wouldn't be slowed down. I switched between the two riding horses regularly because I was riding almost twenty hours a day now.

I was sleeping only four hours each night, and grudgingly at that. Eating mostly jerky because I didn't want to take the time to cook. I was gaining on Oscar again, but my mission now seemed like a grim nightmare. I was driven by thoughts of Anna and the kids and my ranch. I wanted to go home, I just couldn't yet. My mind was constantly on Anna and the kids. Had they made it to the ranch okay? I cursed myself for seven kinds of a fool for sending them out on their own like that. There was no mail service or telegraphs or any way to find out about them, or them about me. I was driven by one thought – the sooner I found and killed Oscar, the sooner I could get home to Anna. I had been driven before, but this was a hundred times more intense.

I began to lose track of time, days blending into each other in what seemed a never-ending stream. My thoughts revolved in continuous circles around Anna and finding Oscar. Grimly I rode on, begrudging every minor slow-down like crossing rivers, circling craters, or backtracking around a cliff, but after several weeks of hard riding I was closing in on Oscar. Funny how knowing his name felt like an accomplishment, when it really didn't mean a thing. I was about two weeks behind him now from the reports I got in towns, and could feel the end of the trail nearing. I believed that soon I would be able to put the dogs on his scent and end this. And then I rode up on a hill and looked down on the remains of a large town. Only one thing could cause that much damage: giants had been here.

After Pa and I had killed that giant on our ranch, people began to kill giants all over, using the machines we built, or copies of them. Pretty soon giants had become more scarce. But the giants weren't completely stupid. They'd figured out that the machine we invented would kill one giant, but take too long to reload to be able to kill a second one, so they started traveling in packs of three or four, and sightings and destruction had begun to increase again. One might get killed right off, but then the rest would destroy the machine and kill everything in sight, smash the buildings, then go on to wreak further destruction elsewhere. Everyone assumed that when they got down to just two left, they would go join another group of giants.

This town I was looking at had been attacked by giants and thoroughly stomped down. Recently. I slowly rode on in. The stench of decaying bodies buried in the rubble of what had once been a town was overpowering. I tied a bandanna around my mouth and nose; I couldn't tell that it helped, but it was somehow a little comforting, so I kept it on. Fires had started during the stomp-down and parts of the town were blackened ashes surrounded by piles of splintered wood. The main street was choked with debris and bloated bodies and the horses had to move slowly and pick their steps. I should have ridden around it, but I thought there was a small chance of finding survivors and helping out. I didn't find anyone until I came to the far edge of the town, and it was just one elderly man. He had moved to the upwind edge where the smell was less intense, and apparently had gotten used to it, but it was still awful strong to me. He told me that his entire family had been killed and that he had no intention of leaving now. He'd dug their bodies out of what was left of his house and buried them, I could see the fresh graves nearby, five mounds in a row with artfully made wooden crosses and names and dates carved in.

I soon heard the whole story, how the giants had come at sunrise two weeks before, how only about a hundred people out of a population of two thousand had survived, and many of those injured, and how they'd pieced together a few wagons and left. The old man told me "We need a better weapon, something that can be fired many times, and rapidly. Otherwise the giants are going to kill us all."

I immediately knew he was right, and within an hour of riding on had figured out a basic concept of how to do it. The problem was that in order to build that new weapon and show other folks how to build more of them, I'd have to give up the trail on Oscar for the better part of three months, maybe longer. And that would delay my killing him, which would delay my getting back home to Anna and the kids. It was obvious from the start what I would decide, but I fooled around for another couple of days pretending I was thinking it over.

I thought about what the old Indian, Big Bear, had said that night in their camp, knowing the right of it, knowing this is what he'd seen when he'd been looking right through me. What I was really doing was reluctantly getting used to the idea of it. I argued with myself that it was not my concern. My concern was killing Oscar and getting home to Anna. I lost the argument because I knew deep down that there are things bigger than us, bigger than our individual lives, and that when called to answer to those kinds of challenges, a man answered. He didn't close his eyes and pretend not to know what he had to do, hard as it might be to do it. The fact that I was not quite sixteen didn't figure into it. I knew how to build a machine that would give us the edge against the giants, knew for certain I could build it, and doubted that anyone else would think of it or know how to build it if they did. It felt like the weight of a thousand giants was on my shoulders, young though they were.

I was as close to Oscar as I had ever been, and thought about finding and killing him and then taking on this larger challenge. Problem was that he could slip away again at any time and I'd have wasted time that could've been spent building the giant-killing machine I had in mind; time that shouldn't be wasted. People all over the country were being killed by giants right now. It wasn't a theoretical problem for them. For them it was life and death; mostly death. It had taken that old man's words to set the inner wheels into motion, but they were in full motion now. I could picture nearly every part of the machine in my mind, and knew I could design the other parts when I had tools in my hands. I was as certain I could build it, and that it would work, as I was of my own name.

I'd need a very good shop to build what I had in mind, one with lots of capabilities. This new weapon was going to be considerably more complicated and harder to build than Pa's first one. I could build it back at home of course, but that would be a long way in the wrong direction as the giants were now mostly up here in the north, and would waste more time getting there, and back to hunt Oscar, than was warranted. Building it by myself would take a year or better, too. I needed help with this to get it done in a short time – a lot of help. I'd heard there was a big steam engine manufacturing plant a couple of hundred miles away in one of the old big cities. Helena, Montana would be something of a ride, but I had been heading that way even while pretending to decide, so I rode on as fast as the terrain allowed.

Two weeks later I rode into Helena. It was as big a city as I had seen in a long time. It was a thriving city, full of people moving around with purpose. I got a hot meal, after that a hotel room, paying extra to keep the dogs with me. I always got a meal first thing when I hit a town – I was hungry most of the time and had gotten thoroughly tired of my own cooking again, when I bothered to cook at all that is. When I had my things in the room, I went looking for the sheriff's office. For the first time in I couldn't remember how long, I left my pistol behind, I felt naked without it, but I wanted to make a good first impression on the sheriff, and walking in with a tricked up fast gun rig would make that damn hard to do. Most of the sheriffs I'd met had not been too friendly once they'd seen what they understood to be a rig designed for a fast draw. I'd given that a lot of thought on the trail, and figured I needed to start off right with Helena's sheriff. Establishing credibility would the first hurdle.

He was a huge and surly looking man with an oddly extra-large head. His features were spread out more than normal and looked kind of distorted. I would bet good money he stopped many a fight just by showing up. He was all business as he asked me what I wanted, barely glancing up at me from his paperwork. He didn't appear to be in a good mood, probably because he had to do paperwork, and he certainly didn't look to be the clerkish type. So I told him in short spare sentences.

"I'm Robert Hunter, my Pa and I built the first machine to kill giants. We killed one on our ranch, the first one ever killed. I passed through a town couple weeks back destroyed by giants and one of the survivors said that a new machine needs to be built. One that can kill multiple giants quickly. I know how to build that machine. I heard there's a good steam shop in this town, and came here to get them to build the new machine. I figured it would be faster if I introduced myself to you, and then you could introduce me to the owner of the factory, since I'll have to take over his shop for a few months. I figure he might resist that idea. You'll want these machines to protect Helena and so you will be persuasive, plus he'll know you, and I'm a stranger to him. And you'll carry the authority of your office with you. He will stand to get incredibly rich, but at first he's only going to see lost profits. My guess is that he would dismiss me out of hand."

The sheriff put down his pen and stared at me for a long moment. "Son, that's a hell of a lot to swallow right there... that surely is. How do I know you are who you say you are, and even then believe you can build this new machine, and after that believe it will work?" He didn't waste words, I noticed that right off.

I was ready for him. I'd been thinking along the trail about credibility, and this very moment. Each night I'd spend an hour or two on a working drawing, showing the principles behind the machine. Campfire living doesn't lend itself to fine detailed drawings, those would come when I got started, so this was a concept drawing with some exploded details around the margins. It was the simplest, clearest and most direct approach I could think of. I didn't need the drawing for myself – I had it all in my head – but showing versus explaining worked tons better for most people. I pulled the drawing from my coat and handed it to him.

He unrolled the drawing on his desk and studied it for a few minutes. "Let's go see Mr. Hauser," he said simply. And we did.

I was right. Mr. Hauser threw out all the objections I had expected. I sat silently as the sheriff was doing a bang-up job of shutting those objections down. The sheriff summarized with, "And as the lad says, you'll get stinking rich building these machines. You'll lose money up front, but the downstream rewards are far more than you are probably imagining right now. Without these weapons, eventually you won't have a factory and there will be no Helena. We're on borrowed time and we both know it. And you've heard of this lad just as I have, as everyone has, he comes from the right background to pull this off." He had unrolled the drawing about mid-way through his pitch and I could tell it had as positive of an effect on Mr. Hauser as it had on the sheriff.

That's when I added my two cents worth. "Pa got rich as hell from our first machine and he wasn't even trying to get rich, he was just trying to help. Imagine what you can do. Oh, and I don't want any of the profits or any pay, just a place to sleep and three meals a day. I've already got more money than I can use." I think that last part may have cinched it.

And so started three months of intense work. Before I got started I asked the sheriff "Do you know of a good trustworthy man that can take a message all the way to west Texas and return with an answer? I can pay him well for the trip."

He did. I met with Joshua that afternoon, and liked him right off. Joshua was a tall young man, slow to talk, but when he talked he made clear sense. He was rawboned from working his own ranch and looked hard as nails. I saw nothing but honesty in his eyes. The amount of money I offered to pay him would set him up on his ranch for years to come. I drew him a map to the ranch and gave him a long letter to Anna, sealed inside a waterproof pouch. He drew half the pay up front and I provided expense money for both legs of travel. He left the next day. I knew it could be two to three months before he returned, so I got busy and tried not to count the days.

The first day in the factory Mr. Hauser called all hands and announced what we would be doing. I could see the men were excited to be part of this. After the introduction I stood up to speak. Jake and

Zeke were, as always, beside me. The men seemed more interested in them than they did me, although no one attempted to pet them. Speaking in front of a crowd was something I had only done once before, and this time it made me purely nervous, but I knew they had to hear from me directly. Once I got started, though, my nervousness fell away because I knew what I was talking about, and I held their attention easily enough.

"Gentlemen, you are looking at a near-sixteen year-old boy and you are wondering. You're wondering if I can make this work or if I'm about to waste all of your time. So first a bit about me." I went on to explain about Pa, our shop, my education, and my ability with machines and the killing of the giant on our ranch. They listened quietly. When I finished that part of my talk I asked for questions. And questions quickly came. They tested me, and tested me hard by asking technical questions about steam engines, thrust calculations, horsepower, machining processes, and torque equations and so on. I answered each question, and the questions eventually died off. They were convinced.

Then I moved on to how this would be organized. "We'll start in the drafting department. With the draftsmen I'll first layout a manufacturing line, and the step-by-step machinery and assembly process. As soon as that's done, you'll begin setting up the equipment, rearranging the shop for maximum efficiency for this application. As you are doing that, the draftsmen and I will be detailing each part of the new machine and the final assembly instructions. You'll be given clear drawings and diagrams with precise dimensions to build from, so that once the fabrication starts it will all flow smoothly to the end product. As soon as the drawings are complete, I'll be out here on the shop floor helping, modifying, improving, and working alongside you."

Then Mr. Hauser stood up and told them that until they were given the drawings it would be business as usual. "But make no mistake, this entire shop will be changed over piece-by-piece to the making of these giant killers. Once production starts in earnest, I'll be instituting a bonus program for maximum production; you'll all be making more money. Now back to work men." Mr. Hauser was a good businessman and knew how to motivate his employees. I saw nothing but smiles as they turned back to work.

And so it went. Bit-by-bit the shop was completely rearranged and the parts manufacturing process began. It was hard work – moving large machines around is an art in itself, combining leverage, rollers, cables and pulleys, and just plain old brute force. Steam pipes had to be dismantled, rearranged for the new locations, and connected. There were times it seemed impossible, but it all finally came together at the end.

Unfortunately, I had become a celebrity in town. I was sleeping in the hotel and eating breakfast and dinner in the hotel's restaurant. Word had spread about what we were doing at the steam shop, and that I was that first giant killer from Texas. People were understandably happy that we would be making the town safe from giants, a worry that everyone had. Word had also spread that the steam plant would be hiring a lot more workers in the near future, a boon for the whole town. People were excited, and I never had a chance to eat alone. Turns out being popular can sometimes be fun, but it can get tiresome as stranger after stranger wants to pump your hand, and no small bunch of them want to tell you about their idea for an invention. I left my handgun in my hotel room, it didn't seem necessary to go around loaded for bear in this town and might just cause some ambitious person to want to try me out. Mostly though the days blurred by in a whirl of activity in the shop.

I rose well before dawn each morning, ate breakfast and then returned to the hotel exhausted late each night. I generally grabbed a quick sandwich at the shop from the lady that came around each noon selling them. Mr. Hauser had set up accounts all over town for me, including the sandwich lady. Physically I was in better shape and better fed than I'd been since I'd started out on the trail. But I missed Anna and the kids something awful, and never fell asleep but that they were the last thoughts I had before sleep struck.

Time went fast and slow at the same time. Each day whizzed by just fine, but the wait for Anna's letter was painfully slow. I'd known it would be of course, but the knowing of it didn't change the feeling of being in cold molasses.

I spent countless hours hunched over a drafting board, meticulously drawing each component of the machine. When each drawing was complete, it was handed over to the two draftsmen to make copies for the shop. My eyes burned and my back ached from hour after hour of drawing. Had there not been such a pressing need on me to get this done I would have taken occasional breaks to straighten up and let my eyes relax, but I was driven, nearly mad with the desire to get this done so I could kill Oscar and then go home.

When I finished the last drawing I shook hands with the draftsmen and congratulated them on their good work, and then I moved myself out onto the shop floor where I worked alongside the machinists. Mostly I coached them on how to make each part, how to set up the raw material and how to drill and grind and hone and measure as they went until the part they were working on was a thing of beauty, a functional piece of art. I insisted that every part be as perfect as man could make it because lives depended on these components. The men were friendly and respectful, but they were also men who worked and lived hard and they gave me as much grief as they gave each other. I in turn gave it right back to them.

The first day in the shop, I was setting up a lathe template. I was sweating and the sweat had been running freely into my eyes. I kept a rag next to me to mop the sweat with. I reached over to grab the rag, without looking as it had become an automatic habit to put it in the same easy to reach spot. Unbeknownst to me a couple of the men had removed the rag and put a stunned garden snake in its place. As soon as my hand landed on the snake, I knew exactly what they were up to. So instead of jerking my hand back I went ahead and grabbed it and took a look at it. I know poisonous snakes quite well, and this was obviously not one. So I coiled it up and then I rubbed the rolled-up snake across my face, turned to the men standing around watching to see how I would react, and said "These yankee snakes don't sop up as much sweat as our Texas rattlers. But if it's the best you got I guess it'll have to do." They about fell down laughing. They whooped and hollered and carried on like kids at recess for a couple of minutes. After that I was one of them.

Not that they didn't still hooraw me after that; in fact they tried harder each time. But it was the same kind of hoorawing they gave to each other all the time. With that one act, I had become the kid brother to every man on the shop floor. They treated me with such a lack of respect that it was a sure sign of high respect and affection. They were good men, each and every one of them, and I enjoyed being around them. I worked as hard as they did, sweated as much as they did, got blisters and then calluses in the same places they had them. We were a family on that shop floor – a motley family to be sure, but a family all the same.

Inside the work shop the work went on like a well-choreographed ballet. Everyone moved in predetermined patterns, and every action was linked to the preceding and the following actions. The music of the shop was all percussive, metal striking metal, sounds of grinding intermixing with different beats from different machine stations. There was a definite rhythm to it all, and that rhythm was felt by the body as much as it was heard by the ears. It was a rough music, brutal to people not used to it, but it was music well understood by the shop's inhabitants.

When a machine malfunctioned anywhere in the shop everyone was aware of it, heard the discordant beat or grind, knew that something had gone wrong. Individual workers on their machines were tightly attuned to the sound of their machine, would hear the slightest difference creeping in. Each machine operator was constantly tuning his machine, as much by ear as by function. When everything was working the way it was supposed to, all were content and the hours flew by each day.

The hours were brutal though, requiring hard muscle work, the shop was hotter than hell and louder than you can imagine. The work was often dangerous, most of the machines had no safety guards on them and a man had to be constantly alert and make every move with care. Too many of the men were missing fingers – but thankfully no one died while I was there. Three men who had been injured too badly to ever work the machines again were taken care of by the others. They donated money to pay for rent and food for these disabled brothers, visited with them often at their home, and when possible the injured would come to the shop for a visit and get a hero's welcome. These were rough men, hard men, but they were men that took care of their own. I found out that Mr. Hauser also quietly paid these men support, but he never talked it up, he just made sure they had all they needed. His men knew that, and the respect he earned was never talked up either, but it was there and it was palpable.

There was still one big hurdle that had to be jumped for the weapon to work. We needed a very high explosive and an inertia-type detonator. I designed the inertia detonator, which was simple enough to build. The explosives though – and they were critical to success – was a daunting challenge. We weren't going to have time to set up an explosives manufacturing process. With time and study I could figure that out, but it was time we didn't have. The giant attacks were increasing in frequency and we needed the solution right away. Once we got the giants on the run we could manufacture our own explosives. Until then we needed some right now.

Mr. Hauser had been working on finding explosives and finally told me that he knew the whereabouts of an old pre-hell storm warehouse that was still full of artillery shells. He thought there were enough explosives in those shells that we might never have to make our own. The next day ten of us rode out of town pulling two wagons loaded with various tools, supplies, food, and eight wagons filled with empty steel drums. It took us three days to find the old military base, which was now filled with crumbling buildings that had trees growing in the middle of some of them. The warehouse was a semi-domed concrete structure that had withstood the ravages of time and neglect better than the other buildings. It had been built far away from the rest of the buildings in case of explosion and held tens of thousands of carefully packed and stored shells. Since the shells were hermetically sealed the explosives inside should still be good. To be sure we carefully disassembled one of the shells, removed the explosives and did a test burn. It was still viable, so we started disassembling the shells in earnest. For this we had to use non-sparking tools, which we'd known before hand and had forged out of brass. Once we got started we melted down most of the tools and re-cast them to fit the exact shape of the components we were working on.

While the men were doing that, I took one of the detonators apart to see if we could use them. Unfortunately, they were too large and too complex to copy in a smaller format. Still, I learned some things I hadn't known before and was thus able to improve my own detonator design. We returned to Helena with ten wagon loads of explosives, leaving the tools behind. A steady caravan of wagons to and from the warehouse began moving as soon as we got back. We'd solved the explosives problem for some time, but eventually Mr. Hauser would have to make his own. He was staying ahead of the curve though, and had spread the word that he needed people schooled in chemistry and was willing to pay good money for their work. Two men had come in together, a father and son that knew their way around explosives, and a shop was being built well out of town for that purpose. That Mr. Hauser never missed a trick.

Joshua finally returned with Anna's letter. Before opening and reading it, I asked Joshua what must have been a hundred questions. He answered each slowly and thoroughly, and I was vastly relieved by his answers. I took the rest of the day off, returned to my hotel room, and read the letter at least a dozen times – actually more than that, I'm sure. They had arrived at the ranch safe and sound, although they'd had a pile of adventures along the way. Anna said that she would tell me all about it in person when I got home. They had planted the garden and it hadn't been but a couple of days before the first of my neighbors had shown up. Good thing I'd given her the introduction letters, she said, because the neighbors went from being about to run them off all the way to being as helpful as you could ask for after reading them.

She was teaching the kids on a daily basis and some of the neighbor's kids had started showing up for lessons, too, bringing various kinds of food and other gifts as payment.

"We've got a regular school going here, with an average of eighteen children in class each day. Getting chores done around the place presents no problem with all these willing hands, and the cattle are being well tended for by just about everyone in the area. The only thing that could make this more of a paradise is you being with me."

I was immensely relieved to hear the good news from home, and with a clear mind I was able to dig deeper and harder every day to get the machines built, operational, and proved. Joshua had also had a few adventures during his travels, but getting him to talk about them was something else again. I did gather that he'd been in several dust-ups along the way, but beyond that no details. He was definitely the type that kept his thoughts to himself, and was able to handle his own problems. With the final payment in hand he returned to his ranch and began making intelligent improvements to his grazing range such as damming a creek for year round water, and spreader dams that slowed rain run-off to allow the water to soak in. That improved the grass on his range. He also bought good breeding stock. He was off to a good start now and I had no doubt that he'd make a great success of it. Best of all he married his sweetheart now that he could assure her of a good life, and I'm certain a big family would be in his future. It was little enough that I did for him in return for what he did for me, and he didn't squander the money, he worked hard and he worked smart.

Three months after beginning we had our first prototype to experiment with. We loaded it up and test fired it successfully on the first try, but I did learn how to improve the cycle rate so those new improvements went back into the system and we began producing two new machines every day. But they still needed to be proven in battle.

We had been monitoring rumors and sightings of giant activity and had settled on a group of them that wasn't too far away. We mobilized with me leading the group. My age had long since stopped bothering the men and they followed willingly. Even Mr. Hauser and the sheriff and the Mayor of Helena came along. As did about a hundred of the town folks, all eager to see this upcoming battle. It would be me and my machine alone against the giants, the rest would have to stay well back in case of failure. I had more volunteers than I could count to be there with me; these were brave folks after all, but I insisted that it was a one man operation and putting other people in danger would be pure wrong. They didn't like it one bit, not one bit, but they grudgingly gave way to my logic and promised to stay back out of harm's immediate way. Truth was that if I failed, they were in grave danger, too, but there was no talking them out of that.

—————◆—————

The scouts we sent out a week ahead trickled back in reporting. We plotted trajectories on a map and decided on an intercept point for the group of five giants. Five would be a hell of a test, dangerous to a fault with only me operating the one machine. Any mechanical failure, any missed shot, any misfire of the explosive charge and I'd be a headless bag of wrinkled skin in seconds. But it would also conclusively prove the concept if it worked. *When it worked,* I kept telling myself. I'd be lying to say I wasn't scared, and I may be many things, but a liar isn't going to be one of them. I owed too much to my parents to darken their name by lying.

I wondered often if I should allow a second machine to be set up for some backup reinforcement, but the truth was that I didn't want to be distracted in the least way when the action started, and I was afraid that another machine firing next to me might be a big distraction. I'd have to be thinking about which giant they were shooting at and whether or not they hit it in order to know where I needed to shoot. No, better by far to know exactly what was happening every second, and the only way to do that was to be the only one shooting.

It took three days to drive the machine into place. We had built a self-powered steam wagon with a low gear ratio and high-traction steel wheels. These were slow-moving vehicles but they had tremendous torque and could travel over almost any terrain. I had chosen a hilltop in the direct line of march of the five giants, about a mile away was another hilltop where the town observers would watch, hidden in a copse of trees. If any of the giants didn't get killed the hope was that the observers would be hidden and thus go unscathed. Our timing was good, I didn't have to wait long, and that was a good thing because waiting seems to bring out every doubt you can imagine – mostly ridiculous doubts, true – but they come unbidden and can crowd the mind and drive it into a frenzy.

Similar to the original one shot machine, this one used compressed steam to drive a flechette inside a sabot. These flechettes were radically different though. Each was a one-inch diameter tube filled with the high explosives and a needle sharp tapered tip of hardened cobalt steel. Inside with the explosives was an inertial detonator. It worked by having a spring loaded firing pin strike a shotgun shell. The spring was pulled back and held by a small latching device which held under acceleration or at rest – but sudden deceleration released it, and then the spring-driven pin would strike the primer which would detonate the shotgun shell and cause the explosives inside the flechette to detonate. My theory was that the flechette would be imbedded inside the giant by the time the explosion went off – and it had worked during mockup testing.

The explosion, I hoped, would do massive internal damage to the giant and also cause a sharp surge of hydraulic pressure throughout the giant's body, rupturing arteries. The theory was sound, but in practice we didn't yet know how fast it would drop a giant – or if it would drop one at all. There was only so much that could be learned by firing at static objects; the effect of the weapon on a living giant could only be tested on a living giant. I had eliminated as many variables as it was possible to eliminate, now it was time to find out if all my theorizing was accurate or not, and it was quite literally a do-or-die test. But if it wasn't tested and proved to kill giants it would be worse than useless.

The machine that fired the flechettes was similar in concept to the Gatling guns of ancient times. It had six barrels that revolved around a central column, each barrel firing one flechette. Rotation was driven by the steam engine's power-take-off and a chain and gear device. The gun was mounted on a tri-pod and had easy-to-use sights. It was fairly mobile, quick to aim and could fire a flechette every 1.2 seconds if need be, taking only that long for the barrels to revolved to the next firing position and for the steam to recharge into the launch tube. It was designed to fire only when the trigger was pulled, allowing for the operator to fire, re-aim and fire again. It could be reloaded in a bit under twenty seconds with six more charges by two trained men working it, but in this kind of battle that was way too long and I didn't want anyone near me to distract me.

The intended purpose of this weapon system was to be used in groups of two or three weapons, each on a separate wagon. Each wagon would hold eighteen additional flechettes and a three-man crew. One man to fire and two men to reload and tend the steam generator. This system could be quickly mobilized by a town to defend itself from approaching giants. And they could be driven cross country should a group want to go on the attack and kill giants in the wilderness. There was every possibility that in the future an army would be assembled to find the giants' home ground and go on the offensive. This weapons system could be instrumental in accomplishing that.

I had an effective range of almost half a mile, and I watched as the giants approached that mark. They came as a group with no particular order to their assembly. They didn't appear to be disciplined at all, just a group moving somewhat loosely together, although they held their line as was usual. The thought occurred to me that maybe they used a form of geomagnetic navigation, like geese do when migrating. That planted an idea way in the back of my mind for a weapon that would disrupt and confuse them by altering the magnetic currents around them. That thought process took less than half a second to flash through my mind, but now wasn't the time to be thinking about it, so I stored it for later.

I would have preferred that they'd been in some kind of formation. That would have made figuring out a firing order simpler; predictability would have been nice. But it was what it was. Even from this distance they were shaking the ground, the combined impact of their ten huge feet rumbling through the earth's crust the way thunder rumbled through the sky in advance of a storm. I wanted to feel that block of ice that I'd felt when confronting those three bad men some months back, but there I'd known exactly what would happen when a bullet entered the men's brains, and I'd been sure I could put those bullets there. Here I still had some doubt as to how effective the explosive charges would be, and I was shooting a round that could be affected by wind, and at a long range. I had doubts, plenty of them, but I guess anyone in that situation would have.

When the first giant reached the boulder I had previously marked as just inside effective range I fired. I watched as the sabot fell away and the flechette carried on. It was moving at a remarkable velocity but given its size I could see it all the way to the target. It took a slightly arching trajectory, rising up as it moved forward, cresting at the mid-point, then moving back down again. The entire flight couldn't have taken more than two seconds, but to me it seemed like two years. I watched the flechette strike the giant dead center of its chest. It was a perfect hit. The flechette disappeared into the giant and there was an immediate eruption of blood and gore that tore out of its body front and back as the charge went off inside its chest cavity. The hydraulic surge ripped out through the top of the giant's head at the same time, making a weird and gory scene that will be in my mind for the rest of my life. It worked! It worked!

Relief tried to mix with the fear that I might miss one of the next four giants – and that relief died a quick death as the remaining giants focused on my position, the cloud of escaping steam making me obvious, and turned and began running right at me. Good Lord but they moved fast, far faster than can be imagined without actually having seen it. Scary fast. One down, four to go, and they were moving in on me as fast as lightning.

I killed the second one and the other three came on at me, but they had changed their tactics somewhat. Instead of coming in a wide line they had fallen into single file. It was an immensely stupid move on their part as I could now hold a steady point of aim and just pull the trigger again as soon as the one in front went down, exposing the next one in line. Had they spread out and run at me in a zig-zag fashion I doubt I could have gotten them all, they covered the ground so fast. The machine was flawless, but the giants were so fast, even coming straight at me as they did, I barely had time to get the last one.

That last one died just yards from me, blowing gore all over me and the weapon and the wagon as the explosive went off. I sat down and started shaking then from adrenaline, and then I vomited. The nasty stuff covering me was repulsive and nauseating and stank like the inside of a ten day-old cow lying in the hot sun. Putrid doesn't begin to cover it. I stripped my clothes off and wiped down best I could with some rags in the wagon box. I could hear faint cheering from the observers but I felt sick from the adrenaline. I shakily walked down to the creek at the bottom of the hill and washed off, standing there naked as the day I was born as the town people came rushing up. I was too sick to be embarrassed. They quickly found me a change of clothes and brought them to me, but they were slapping me on my bare back the whole time. I'd never seen such happy people.

This is not something I wanted to do every day. I couldn't wait to get away from them and back on Oscar's trail. Knowing this, I'd brought all my things with me, including my three horses. Jake and Zeke of course had been beside me the whole time, bravely snarling and barking at the giants as they charged our position, and if ordered to I had no doubt they would have attacked the giants, but it would have been like fleas attacking an elephant.

Of course the town folks argued until they were all blue in the face about me leaving. They wanted me to come back to town, to be the hero, to partake in the several days of celebration that were coming, to lead a parade. But I declined, thanked them kindly, but firmly declined. I had to find and kill Oscar so I could get home to Anna. They were still standing in a clump looking disappointed as I crested the far ridge and looked back. I almost felt bad about not going with them, but they'd get along just fine without me and I'd not spare another second in my search. I'd given them what they needed, proven it worked, and left them in excellent shape to make more of the machines. My part in the big picture of the giant war was done, or so I thought at the time, and I had pressing business to get back to. I waved, they all waved back, and I rode out of sight.

I was at long last back to hunting Oscar. I rode back to the last point I'd been at, the giant-stomped town, and began the search again from there. I found the old man's desiccated body, he'd dug a grave next to those of his family, lain down in the open hole, and shot himself in the chest. I filled the grave in for him below the marker he'd made for himself. It was a sad and depressing morning. And I had an inkling of how he felt being bereft of his family. I said the words over him that the preacher had said over my folks, then moved back to the hunt.

I had believed I was within a couple of weeks of catching up to Oscar the last time I was here, and now I was at least four months behind. In fact I had completely lost the trail. Based on his previous travel direction I moved on, asking questions. Eventually I picked up a hint of the trail again, but it was faint, just a whisper, not even climbing the scale to a rumor.

I began to wonder if maybe I was going about this the wrong way, this was in an inefficient way to find someone – and where before I had been driven to find him I hadn't been in a tearing rush about it, I was now. I wanted to find him and end this, and I wanted to end it as soon as possible. Each new day brought a growing sense of unease in me. I began toying with the idea of trying to outguess where he might go, so I got out my map and began plotting a path. I'd followed him long enough to know that he mostly avoided larger cities, preferring smaller towns. I traced out where I'd had confirmation of his presence in the past and looked for a pattern. Other than a more or less meandering line from south to north and then a gradual swing to the east there didn't appear to be a pattern. I also considered how he financed himself. For a long time he had been plush with Pa's gold coins, and he spent them, but fairly sparingly. When would he run out? What would he do then? Turn to crime again I knew. I went ahead and plotted where I thought he would most likely go and put the map away.

That night I had a nightmare, a bad one. I woke up in the dark in a heavy sweat with my heart beating in my chest like an earthquake. I had a sudden fear brought to the surface by the dream. And if that fear became reality, a nightmare would indeed be my life, and worse, Anna's. I saddled my horse, kicked dirt over the dying coals, and headed for Texas. In the dream, Oscar had run out of gold, thought there must be more at the ranch somewhere, and had returned there finding Anna and the kids, and began torturing them for the location of the hidden gold.

I realized I had unwittingly sent Anna into a potential death trap. I'd never hated myself until that moment, and I thoroughly despised myself for being so blind stupid. I had placed hate, the hate for Oscar, above love for Anna. Stupid, stupid, stupid. I had been stupid to think that killing Oscar was more important than protecting Anna. I was stupid to think that everything would be just hunky-dory while I traipsed around the country weeks and months behind the killer. I'd turned seventeen two weeks before but I'd been a boy, thinking like a boy, acting like a boy. I'd thought of my own needs first and had ignored the real need, the only need that mattered, the need to protect those that I love. I grew up a lot that night. I realized that while I had believed myself to be mature, I'd actually been caught in immaturity's own worst trap, putting ego over necessity. In a matter of seconds I realized how foolish and stupid I was, and that I might already be too late, he might already have been there for all I knew.

As I rode that night I thought more about it. Petty crime wouldn't be his style anymore; he had grown accustomed to having gold and drifting from town to town, driven by the inner demons that only he knew. Robbing people in alleys, or holding up banks would make his trail hot and he knew it. He didn't know that I was on his trail as I hadn't gotten close enough for him to know, and he hadn't backtracked across his own trail even once that I was aware of, but he was naturally cautious and covered his trail instinctively. He wouldn't draw attention to himself any more than he had to, or than a sudden rage would cause. I was as sure as the knowledge of the next sun rise that he would eventually think to go back for more gold, if he hadn't already. Problem was that I wouldn't know when the thought would strike him. Anger at myself spurred at me as hard as the fear for Anna's safety did.

I traveled almost twenty four hours a day getting home. I bought two more horses, I had four total now. I switched horses every four hours and would have gone on without stopping at all, but the horses and the dogs needed sleep. I could sleep in the saddle, they couldn't. I stopped when I had to for them, grudgingly I'll admit, for the need to get home was sorely on me. I traded for fresh horses along the way when I could, always anxious to make the deal and get moving. I gladly paid far more in the trades than reason would have allowed, but my reasons had nothing to do with the fair price of horses.

Riding so hard and being so exhausted led me to make a stupid mistake. I had become numb to my surroundings, no longer alert to danger, and because of this I rode right into a camp of renegades. Tired and exhausted as I was I'd missed any signals that Jake and Zeke might have given me. I was riding at close to a gallop as I came busting out of the trees and into the small crater where they were camped. And just like that I was in the middle of a group of men, all shooting at me. I felt a bullet pluck at my sleeve and then my pistol was out and blazing away. Jake and Zeke attacked and had two of the renegades down in a second. I had to wheel the horse after the man on my left went down, then I fired two more shots into a second man. Turning the string of horses around would take way too long so I charged on right through the middle of them, shooting right and left as I spurred my horse and quickly disappeared from their sight into the trees across the meadow with Jake and Zeke right behind me, guarding my retreat. I wasn't even sure how many of them there were, it happened that fast and the light was getting bad.

Once in the trees I stopped long enough to reload, check myself for injuries of which I found two bullet grazes that had burned the skin only. They were barely bleeding. I was barely breathing from the sudden shock of it all. Luckily none of the horses or Jake or Zeke had been hit. Those men were in as much shock as I was and didn't pursue, and I didn't wait around for them to settle their thoughts. I rode on, fast.

The whole thing couldn't have lasted over fifteen seconds, but I bet that story got told around a lot. "They're we were, sitting around the fire and drinking a little, out in the middle of nowhere when all of a sudden three men and a pack of wolves charged right out of the trees, attacked us, then rode on as fast as they rode in. Lost three men to bullets, lost one to the wolves, and three more were badly torn up. Couldn't have lasted more than three or four seconds from beginning to end. Damndest thing I ever saw and I've been around some."

Jake and Zeke were getting down to skin and bones and must have often thought of abandoning me, but they stuck, and ran, and suffered painfully. Their poor paws were raw and bleeding when we finally reached the ranch. I fed them every night along the way, but I had no appetite for eating and only choked down a few mouthfuls every night because I knew I needed it in order to keep going, but it all tasted like ashes. I lost weight, saw my reflection in a pond I was drinking from and didn't recognize the gaunt, haunted-looking young man with deep dark eye sockets looking back at me. It took me five weeks. Five weeks of feverish hell, tormented by thoughts of what could or might have happened to Anna and the kids. Sleep evaded me for the most part, but when I did sleep it was worse than being awake and I got no rest from that horror-filled nightmarish sleep.

When I rode into my yard at last I was a sorry sight. I had lost a lot of weight and without my shirt my ribs poked out. I hadn't bathed in weeks, I stank, and a partial beard had finally started to grow so my face was scraggly-looking. I had a dangerous and desperate look about me, and wouldn't have been at all surprised to see Anna come out the door with a shotgun leveled, both barrels cocked and fear on her face.

But I was wrong. She saw me through the window and recognized me, came out whooping and hollering and laughing fit to beat the band, with the kids surging out around her and the little one scooting between her legs. It was a glorious homecoming. Pleasure and relief mixed with a renewed feeling of love as I saw her happy and healthy face. I nearly sobbed with relief, tears making trails through the dirt on my face. When Anna got a good look at me she suddenly looked scared, scared that I would fall down dead right then and there. Scared that I had lost my mind and had become a raving lunatic. It took some talking to calm her down again, and once she saw I was healthy enough, and sane enough, she bloomed all over again.

Anna and the kids had arrived at the ranch safe and sound, but the trip had been quite an adventure and she'd had to pull her pistol twice. I think it was the first time she had begun to realize just how beautiful she is. Having been raised in the wilderness and hardly ever seeing other people hadn't given her a sense of how men would react to seeing her. On the trip south she found out, and while it was funny as hell to listen to her talk about it, I could tell that she had been deeply disturbed to have been the cause of so much ruckus. She is naturally shy, would have been shy even if she'd been raised in a city, and the attention she'd received over and over again on the trip wasn't welcome. Apparently she didn't have any problem displaying her displeasure over it either. I tried hard to keep a straight face, but in the end I had to laugh. Thank heavens she laughed with me. I'd not want to rile her up; I might not be able to get out of it uninjured.

We sat up all night. Bad as I needed sleep, there was just no way I was sleeping that night, so we sat on the porch in the rocking chairs, just talking. The kids tried to hang on, but one by one they dropped off to sleep right there on the porch. Not one of them would go inside. We watched the sun come up holding hands and grinning like young apes. It was a short, but wonderful homecoming.

As soon as the first of the kids stirred Anna and I began packing the wagon. I was taking her to Abilene, a four day trip by wagon. Abilene was a medium small town that had a good sheriff, good hotel, and importantly in my mind, a decent restaurant.

None of them wanted to go, knowing I was coming back alone. But I explained to them what I thought would happen when Oscar showed up at the ranch, as I was now certain he would, and that each of them was a potential hostage or target. I explained that I couldn't fight effectively if I had them to worry about too. I explained that if they stayed they put me in danger, not to mention the danger they'd be in. Eventually they reluctantly agreed, and off to Abilene we went. I slept soundly each night of the trip, and ate great quantities of food, as if I'd been starved for years. The dogs were so paw-sore that I made them ride in the wagon with the kids, and the kids gave them lots of attention and fed them a lot, too.

When we got to Abilene I settled my family – that's how I thought of them now, and they of me – in the hotel, paying a healthy bonus for allowing the dogs to stay with the kids. I knew Jake and Zeke would be extra protection for Anna and the kids, and could inadvertently give me away to Oscar when I waited for him if I took them back to the ranch with me. I went to the restaurant and quietly paid the owner a nice bonus for taking extra special care of my family. I'd given Anna enough gold to buy rooms and meals for a year, I didn't think it would take that long, but I wasn't going to leave them short either. I then visited the sheriff and explained what I was doing, and why. He said he understood me doing it and wished me luck. He volunteered to keep a close eye on my family while I was gone. He also made a suggestion that hadn't occurred to me, so my next errand was to the town's lawyer.

I had him draw up a will that left the ranch to Anna if I lost the fight. With all that taken care of, I made a sad farewell to the kids, then a sadder one to Anna. I'd lie if I didn't say she wanted to leave the kids and come with me; she made a pretty strong argument for it, too, and almost had me swayed. But not quite enough. I saddled up, told Jake and Zeke to stay with Anna, and rode home, taking two days for the trip at top speed.

When I got home, I didn't ride right up to the

house. I came in quietly in the dark and picked a spot with a good view of the buildings. Then I waited all day, just observing. He wasn't there yet. After dark that evening I went to the house and gathered what I needed. Binoculars, food, ammo, a bedroll, coffee and coffee pot and a skillet, canteens, rifle. I returned to my vantage point. It was a good one, with a small, cave-like area beneath some boulders that would keep me dry, shaded, and well-hidden. Then I began the long wait.

And long it was. I had no idea when Oscar would show up, but I remained dead certain that he would. In the meantime, I had plenty of time to think about where I'd come from, what I'd been doing, and whether or not I was doing the right thing. Occasionally I would go down to the house after dark to stock up again. I cooked once a day in my camp, but made coffee more often, cooking over a very small, nearly smokeless fire of extremely dry wood. Because I had stacked rocks up high around it and positioned it in the place of maximum camouflage, you couldn't see the fire at all unless you were inside the cave with it.

After the first two days of watching the grass not grow, I fetched some books and spent a lot of time reading. I had chosen philosophy as the subject; seemed like the right place and time for such reading. I studied on the subject hard, too, and spent many an hour pondering those imponderable questions. In the end I learned what I had already been taught by my parents, to do what you believe is right and proper given the circumstances you find yourself in. Millions of words wandering thousands of paths had been written on the topic, and it was really just that simple. Simple, but sometimes it took a huge amount of courage to do the right thing.

My vantage point was high enough to view much of the surrounding country, sometimes for as far as the eye could see. It was easy weather and that was a blessing. On the first day of the fifth week I spotted a faint trace of smoke from the north east, someone had a camp fire out there. I felt a surge of adrenaline. I knew it was Oscar; it had to be him. I'd not get any sleep that night.

It was near noon by the shadows when he came riding in. He wasn't making any attempt at being coy about it, just rode right in without any sign of caution or fear. I saw him coming from several miles away and made my way down to the barn. I could have picked him off easily with a rifle, but I wanted to see his face up close, identify the scar. I'd make no mistake about who I shot, and when I got up close enough to see the scar, I would only need my pistol.

I wanted revenge. And I believed that revenge was right and proper under these circumstances and to hell with those philosophers that thought revenge was wrong – they were wrong, just plain wrong. Revenge has its time and place, too. I also wanted a life with Anna that didn't include worrying about this man showing up in it whenever he damn well pleased. I searched deep and found no trace of reluctance, nor did I find any hint that there would be regret later. I wasn't hyped up on adrenaline now, either, just a calm resolution to see this through. That icy calm had returned with a vengeance.

As he stepped out of the saddle in front of my house, I walked out from behind the barn; we were less than fifty feet apart. I kept walking; this was to be close work, I wanted it personal. I saw the scar, and he fit the description perfectly. Given that, and the fact that he was at my house as I had predicted, there was no chance I would be killing the wrong man. None.

He saw me right away of course and stepped away from his horse, stood stock still facing me as I approached. I walked right up to him and slapped him hard across the face, hard enough to momentarily buckle his knees, then I took two steps back, right into the front edge of my sweet spot. He was shocked, had never in a million years expected that slap, hadn't even put an arm up to block it. He was instantly outraged, his lips pinched and white and his hands trembling. I guess he had never been treated that way before in his life and it shook him to his core. Being treated like that by a boy, it just wasn't his image of himself as a bad man.

"Oscar" I said. The low menace in my voice surprised me, it sounded like an adult's voice. I saw the recognition of his own name. "This is my home. I was away when you murdered my parents, but I've been waiting for you. This is the moment when you die, that moment you've always been afraid of. I'm going to kill you."

He didn't hesitate once he realized just what the hell was going on. He reached for his pistol and he was damn fast, his hand just a blur. He wasn't fast enough though, it wasn't even a contest. I'd grown far faster since Mr. Wurther's lessons, and I'd been fast then. My first bullet hit him in the solar plexus. I could have head shot him as easily, but I still had something to say and I wanted him to live just long enough to hear it. I wanted the hatred in my voice to be the last thing he ever heard.

"That one was for Pa." I said. Oscar's body had wrenched up tight when my bullet had torn through his chest, his gun hand faltered and he fired into the dirt between us.

"This one is for Ma." I shot him in the face, just like he had her. He fell dead instantly, only a couple of feet from where I had found Pa's body.

I walked back to my cave, gathered the remaining food, walked back to the barn and saddled my horse and rode over to the body. I dismounted and tied a rope around his ankles, tied the other end to my saddle horn, stepped into the saddle and started riding towards Abilene dragging the inert carcass behind. He didn't deserve a burial and he wouldn't get one. After I was well off our property, I turned south a few miles and dragged the body up onto a large flat rock where the buzzards would soon enough find it. I found it fitting to think of Oscar being turned into buzzard dung. I untied the rope from my saddle and let it drop.

Then I sunk spur for Abilene. I had a wedding to attend.

Made in the USA
San Bernardino, CA
15 May 2015